SHIKSA

Praise for David R. Slavitt

[Slavitt's] sentences are so unburdened by the trivial or any kind of distraction, so transparent, that it would be too gross even to say that they are like angels in the sky. Because they don't just hang around in the sky like angels; they *are* the sky. They are not merely fluent, though fluency is hard to come by and something to be treasured; they flow as unhaltingly as a creek or waterfall. If I compare Slavitt's sentences to natural phenomena, it may be because he himself is rather a natural phenomenon: a man who writes easily, copiously, and beautifully.

KELLY CHERRY, author of *A Kind of Dream*

He is an extraordinarily learned writer, intimate with the best literature of the Western tradition from the poets of the Greek Anthology to the contemporary poets whose translations he has edited for the Pennsylvania series of Greek tragedies and comedies. None of it is lost on him. The great works have worked upon him, and this is one of his means of achieving greatness.

DANIEL MARK EPSTEIN, author of *The Ballad of Bob Dylan*

The name of David R. Slavitt may not yet be one to conjure with in literary circles, although if he were a magician, let's say, or a juggler, his skill in keeping so many poems, novels, translations, and other works in the air would have drawn gasps of astonishment and awe, as he added title upon title until he has now tossed out for our enjoyment *over 100 books.*

JOHN M. RIDLAND, author of *Fires of Home*

Slavitt is a master satirist, whose elegant, irreverent prose is full of witty quotations that we want to read aloud to friends.

Philadelphia Inquirer

Shiksa

David R. Slavitt

C&R PRESS

PRESS

Shiksa © 2014 by David R. Slavitt

FIRST EDITION PAPERBACK

ISBN-13: 978-1-936196-41-8
ISBN-10: 1-936196-41-7
LCCN: 2014931877

Cover design by Aggie Toppins
Book design by Terrence Chouinard
The typeface is Scala.

...on your rosebud lips where often I
have drunk thirsty for more of what I was having,
my greedy soul both feared and longed to die.

Charles-René Marie Leconte de Lisle

Say I'm weary, say I'm sad,
Say that health and wealth have missed me,
Say I'm growing old, but add,
Jenny ssed me.

James Henry Leigh Hunt

1

I COULD GIVE MYSELF A NAME, but I know that would be of no effect. Readers will assume that it's me. If I change my name as the writer, I have a *nom de plume,* but then if I use my real name in the book, is that a *nom de guerre?* A binomial equation. (I haven't thought of them for years, nor have they thought of me.) So a narrator appears, at least for confusion's sake so that readers might not be sure whether he or the protagonist is a version of the author. His intermediation would not be for the purpose of relating some pseudo biographical narrative but simply to obfuscate and show how all narrations are misrepresentations. It is, at any rate, a painful story and I'd rather somebody else tell it, despite the fact (or because of it) that it's my life.

But I have no life except for what little I can remember. The rest, most of it, is what I imagine or invent to fill the gaping lacunae. This would not be so disturbing (to me) if I had any idea which were memories and which were fabrications. Or wishes or fears. And none of these is any more real than the others. He can be helpful because he has no life at all.

To call the narrator David would be perverse (amusing, too, but not enough). Marcel? Same thing, but too cute. I'll work on it and I promise to keep you posted.

WHAT OBTAINS? I'm seventy-eight years old and ought to have at least a vague idea of how to manage these things. Actually, I will be 78 in a few weeks. I'm 'going on' 78, as we used to say when we were five or six. We wanted the next number, which would get us a little closer to adulthood and independence (or so we assumed). I use it because it's a scary number that I am hoping to ease into as one eases into a cold swimming pool, toe, foot, other foot.... Plunging in would be better but that takes physical courage. And as I get older and more experienced, my confidence deserts me. I am ever more tentative. The basics of life that I took for granted as a young and then a middle-aged man seem ever less reliable.

'Call me Ishmael,' Melville begins. Right there, in the third word, there's a name. Here I am on the third manuscript page and I'm still dangling that toe just over the surface of the glittering, cold, too green, too chlorinated water.

Call me Starbuck? I'm drinking coffee, after all.

ROMAIN, MAYBE? As in Gary? The name means novel, and that has a piquancy he never exploited, so far as I know. He was married for a while to Jean Seberg and before that to Leslie Blanche. He wrote some novels few people now read, despite his having won the Prix Goncourt (twice). Seberg committed suicide, as did he, and he left a note saying that his suicide had nothing to do with hers. (Was he worried about being charged with plagiarism?) Heaven forefend.

One of his novels was *Roots of Heaven*.

GARY WOULD WORK, but may be too obvious. At one further remove, there is Kacew, which was Gary's real name. It's pronounced Ketzev. And in Jewish tradition, anyone who sneezes is believed to have spoken the truth. In France it sounded foreign, which is probably why he changed it. (And then, perversely, he occasionally used it as a pseudonym. *Nom de Dieu!*)

We'll see how it feels as we go on. After all, I can always change it. One difference between fiction and life is that, in the latter, you can never go back to correct things.

Kacew did use other names, like Shatan Bogat and Fosco Sinibaldi. That last one has a certain sinister charm. Would you not be uncomfortable if your daughter turned up with a boyfriend bearing that name? You are a liberal person, or you think you are, and what difference would it make? It would depend on what kind of person he was, right? What's in a name, as Shakespeare asked, stringing together an endless series of catch phrases and book titles to make his plays?

Most of the time, I might concede that you have raisins, but here, when the name is all we have, it's . . . all we have. We could describe him, or, more accurately, give him one of those boilerplate descriptions nineteenth century novelists worked on. (And we read them, of course, but we can't actually visualize the character from what the authors have told us, can we? It was a convention, merely. The novelists had described and the reader, therefore, supposed himself to be satisfied.)

You want that? I can provide that: 'He was a handsome man—if an old man near seventy may be handsome—with grey hair, bright keen eyes, and arched eyebrows, with a well-cut eagle nose, and a small mouth, and a short dimpled chin. He was under the middle height, but nevertheless commanded attention by his appearance. He wore no beard save a slight grey whisker, which was cut away before it reached his chin. He was strongly made, but not stout, and was hale and active for his age.'

Okay? It's as good as Trollope. Actually, it is. I refrain from the snotty 'as you will recall,' but it's from *Sir Harry Hotspur of Humblethwaite*. I don't understand the 'slight grey whisker' but I don't mind not understanding it. We learned as children to accept some things on faith. Most things, actually. Anyway, that's what Kacew might as well look like. He speaks in one of those indefinable accents that refugees sometimes have, slightly nasalized and with very precise elocution. British but not quite—not out of any Anglophilia but only to preen a little. Elocution as haberdashery. (Bespoke speech!) So he sounds the way Nabokov did. (NaBOHkov, as he insisted.)

We could tinker with the description if we wanted to. Let's make him a little taller, perhaps. I think the point of the 'under the middle height' was to depart if only slightly from an excessively idealized look, and maybe to set up for the way he 'nevertheless' could command attention.

Of course, he commanded attention. Eponymous characters in novels often do. And narrators, too. Especially if the novel is in any way interesting.

So he's taller. Five, eleven, say. Does that make him more vivid or less? Is it better this way or this way? (Have you ever thought about what sex with an optometrist must be like?) No? Ah, but now you have. And do you like it better this way?

THE STORY IS THAT Maxwell Perkins cut the first sixty pages or so of *The Sun Also Rises* and in the middle of page 67, say, made a line with a grease pencil across the page (Black? Red? Stendhal would have known.), writing STORY STARTS HERE in big block letters. What I've heard is that those pages were a description of how Barnes got his wound. Better not to know? Or did Perkins, who was something of a priss, just feel uncomfortable about it. It was a groinish sort of wound, after all.

Anyway, in Kacew's nasalized voice, 'Story starts here.'

You will have noticed that so far there hasn't been any story at all. It has taken all this time to establish, name, and describe a narrator, which is admittedly languid. Oblomovian, almost. (Goncharovian?) The author is perhaps too tentative. Or uncertain. Or reluctant? Afraid, more likely. In fact, both of us are dummies, speaking whatever words the inner ventriloquist prompts. It's quite an act. I sit on his lap while he sits on that of the ventriloquist, who is invisible and unknowable. We draw inferences and make guesses (this is literary criticism, no?) but we can't know. It is, in part, his mysteriousness that makes him interesting. Marxists, Freudians, deconstructionists, cultural historicists, and all the other literary fauna take their best shots, but where they fail is that they are uncomfortable with mystery. And randomness. They are left as befuddled as the earnest students in front of them.

Take my name. (Please, as Henny Youngman would say.) We watched it develop from Romain, but the author neglected to tell us that he had read a review of an exhibition of Roman Vishniac's photographs somewhere. And that set him off woolgathering about how Vishniak is a kind of cherry brandy, and that Roman vishniak would probably have been aged in cherry wood barrels while the Warsovian variety would be served raw, right out of the still with a burn to it that the Poles settle for and even claim to like. (This is not true but who cares?) What is more important is that it went nowhere. Still the name remained, rattling around in the gourd of his deliberately empty mind. Roman, I mean. That's how Gary popped up. He hadn't thought of Gary in decades. (Who has?)

So, you see, one odd thing leads stupidly but inevitably to the next. (Everything in the past appears to have been inevitable.) But having figured that out we are no further along the path to understanding than we were before. The mind works in peculiar ways, but the world, too, may function according to such unprincipled principles. My guess (Kacew!) (Gezundheit!) is that external reality, which claims to be authoritative, makes no sense either but does so in an altogether different way, so that a glint of light in one domain does not illuminate anything in another.

He hadn't thought of Lesley Blanche, either, who wrote *The Wilder Shores of Love*. He read that when it came out but doesn't remember much about it except that he liked it.

Which may offer an answer to the difficult conundrum Protestants have been fretting about. You cannot earn your way into heaven. I've mentioned Gary's *The Roots of Heaven* but not that Blanche wrote *Sabres of Paradise*. Do they go together? Probably not.

LOOK BACK ON YOUR LIFE. Consider the turning points, the decisions you made and regret. What you had in mind and how it came out in the end bear little relationship to each other. Stuff happens. Who could have imagined that Lesley Blanche would make an appearance here? Not the narrator, nor the author, nor even the ventriloquist—to whom we pay attention in an odd way, not caring much about what he says but only checking to see that he doesn't move his lips. This is a situation Aristotle was too reasonable to address. (Of course, there were no ventriloquists back then.)

Love is the conventional subject for novels and is interesting because it is, as most of us will agree, irrational. The plotting of most novels is depressingly orderly and stays within a predictable framework. (Will she marry the rich cad or the poor but honest fellow who will turn out in the last chapter to be the heir of a distant uncle of vast wealth? The heroine's belief in the fairness of the universe is confirmed, although ours may be stretched a little.) It might be better if the impecunious but worthy young man turns out to have genital herpes. That would be closer to how the world works but probably distressing to readers and a provocation of rage in editors who understand that the only reality of novels is that they are supposed to make money. They may be unlike life or not, make a certain degree of sense or not, but whatever else they do they must earn out their costs. [And woe to any author whose previous book didn't sell well enough to break even.]

I (Kacew) will not have to try too hard to avoid making sense, which, as you have probably figured out, is not my forte. A straw for which a drowning man was grasping is blown by an ill wind to light on the camel's heavily laden back just as he is getting his nose in under the tent flap or trying to squeeze through the eye of the needle (actually a narrow gate in the walls of Jerusalem) and where are you then? Exactly!

So love, because it affects (afflicts?) young men and women who don't know anything. They have their lives in their hands but haven't noticed the stenciled warning labels: FRAGILE, HANDLE WITH CARE, THIS END UP, SIGNATURE REQUIRED. They drive as if there were no tomorrow (for some of them there won't be). Their behaviors invite calamity—which is, of course, our real subject. Not just readers and narrators but every one of us. Every man Jack. Everyman Jack. Every man named Jack. Of all trades. Nimble and quick. And on the spot—except that that's Johnny, which is supposed to be short for Jack.

STORY STARTS HERE.

Or at least we'll give it a shot. Young man, twenty say, bright but stupid. (All twenty-year-olds are stupid.) He knows nothing about life because the expensive education his parents have worked hard to provide for him has been designed to keep him ignorant about anything that matters. An all boys' boarding school? An all men's college? How is he to meet girls, learn how to talk to them, and discover that they are not merely sexual objects but people, too? How is he to learn to be comfortable in their company? He is not alone in these disabilities. All his classmates, indeed, his entire generation—or the best and brightest of them—had the same limitations.

There were parietals. Undergraduates these days don't even know what the word means. (They could look it up but they dislike doing that, taking offense at any word the don't already know. They don't know how to write in cursive script, either, but that's another matter.) You could get thrown out of school for having a female in your room after eight PM. The idea was to discourage sexual intercourse. It didn't. It promoted homosexual sex, although that couldn't have been the intention. And among heteros, the clever ones figured out relatively quickly that they could fornicate in the afternoon and have dinner later. (It's a nice way to do it, actually.) Perversely, the rules forbidding sex in the evening only served to make it more glamorous, more attractive (as if that were necessary). There was a fleabag hotel across the street from campus—the Lincoln Hotel, I think it was—that catered to students. No actual fleas, but dingy, and smelling slightly of disinfectant. One had to climb a brown, mucid staircase to get to the reception desk on the second floor. The Taft, across the street, was much nicer, but they maintained a reputation for vigilance so that nobody wanted to risk being humiliated by a hotel detective, while the Lincoln was cheerfully indifferent. A strange background for the sexual adventures of these upper-middle-class kids. Other than sitting at a table in a hamburger joint, where else could they go to talk after eight o'clock? So they'd repair to the Lincoln. And they could continue their intercourse, sexual and otherwise, as long as they liked. Or play cards, for God's sake.

Back at prep school, the rumor was that they put saltpeter in the mashed potatoes because it was an anaphrodisiac. Some guys therefore avoided the mashed potatoes; others took extra helpings as if to demonstrate that their libidos were strong enough to be impervious to any chemical discouragement. One of the best secondary schools in the country, it seems to have been run by lunatics and designed to wreck the lives of their bright charges. Their success in this enterprise can be measured in the rates of divorce, alcoholism, and depression in their alumni, distressingly higher than those of the general population.

But to hell with sociology. This is fiction, which has its own business to transact. In any event, our protagonist is a special case. Not only has he been in training for awkwardness with girls, but he also has the extra disadvantage of being younger and smaller than most of his classmates. And strenuously unathletic. So he had few friends in prep school, where athletic ability and a delight in horseplay were rewarded. To display any intellectual excellence was bad form. As he found out, soon enough.

DO WE REMEMBER BEING TWENTY? Of course not. I am a figment and was never twenty, but for you, at best there are glimpses. And most of you were so witless at that age as to defy the conventions of narrative. Motivation involves the use of the frontal lobe: if I do this, than that may very well follow. But twenty-year-olds don't bother with such tediousness. Oh, some of the women do, because sooner or later they may want to get married, which is often in their thoughts as they look around at the available possibilities and calculate what they hope for and what they might settle for. But the guys are lolling in the present moment. No past, no future. Scarcely any idea of these intellectual categories. They can think ahead maybe until next Saturday and their hopes are simply to get drunk, to get laid, or, ideally, both.

It's not like that anymore? I have no idea. I'm talking about fifty or sixty years ago, and our protagonist is as much a creature of his times as any of us were or are. This may explain some things but doesn't excuse them.

WE SEE HIM CROSSING A QUADRANGLE, a skinny, slightly gangly kid in khakis, white bucks (no kidding) and a gray, Shetland crewneck sweater. Could use a haircut, maybe, but otherwise he's presentable enough. (Is he short on cash or trying to look Byronic?) If Trollope were here to describe him, he'd point out that the ears stick out from the head a little too much, but that would probably be a craftsmanly touch just to make it clear that it's not just the boilerplate to which we are invited to contribute whatever image we can conjure up.

One wants to call out to him: 'Shmuck! Pay attention! It's your life you are playing with, and you're not very good at the game and even seem not to understand the rules.'

But he doesn't stop or look around. You can't talk to the past, which is grossly unfair because it keeps yammering in your ear with accusations and reproaches. It is impossible to warn him: 'You'll find out, dimwit, and it'll be too late, because it always is.' The most you can do is wait until he is older and then tell him, if you are heartless enough to do it, 'I told you so.'

In any event, his inadequate answer would be that he was doing the best he could with what he had and what he knew at the time. Therapists say things like that, crazy doctors. The idea of actions having consequences was, for him, just literary theory. Or physics. Or philosophy. (None of those was his major.) Still it wasn't altogether his fault because, in the protected existence he had led, nothing bad had ever happened to him—like the death of a parent or even major surgery. He'd always been lucky, getting into the right schools, doing well, and being told how promising he was. If you're on a streak, your bet should be that it will continue, even though the probabilities of the future have no relation whatsoever to happenings in the past. Wall Street brokers have to put that disclaimer in their pamphlets, and what it signifies is that the nice upward graphs in pretty colors don't mean a thing. (It can work the other way, though. Slots players watch the machines and look for a long series of losses, which they think means that the machine is 'ripe.' But it isn't.)

None of this matters. Take it as a given that he was clueless and thoughtless. He may not have been any worse than other young men of his generation, his 'cohort' as they say, but all that means is that they were all guilty. And some of them (only some!) were punished for it.

Can we hang him now? Or do we have to try him a little?

I must keep calm. That's my primary job as a narrator. *Narrador,* working as close to the bull as I can without getting gored. ¡Olé!

(Did you know that that Spanish cheer for bullfighters comes from the Arabic cry of 'Allah'?)

STORY STARTS HERE, God damn it.

It will. In a moment. I promise. (I would swear on my mother's grave, but fictions don't have mothers.) But before it does, I might observe that in most novels, an alert narrator would probably have exploited those ears a little more, might even have used them as a piece of machinery to suggest something of the protagonist's idea of himself. That would have been an efficient piece of business. The ears are not particularly prominent anymore but they were years ago when he was little. He thought he looked like Alfred E. Neuman in *Mad Magazine*. Had he been taunted by his elementary-school classmates about his ears? He can't remember. The narrator is, nonetheless, free to suppose so, on the flimsy pretext that he can't remember *not* being taunted, but then who would? In any event, the ears went with his being under-age and under-sized and they were one more disability. Related to Jewishness? (Neuman, obviously, was Jewish, and the name was/is funny because Alfred is aggressively goyish. He has grown, of course, is almost six feet tall now, and his head has grown, too, so that the ears are not the first thing one notices about him. (Is that why his hair is a little longer than was then fashionable?) But long after the river has run dry, the empty wadi remains to mark the landscape. The nomads know where it is and use it as a landmark, but for mental topography the terra is mostly incognita. Not even the protagonist would be able to make the connection, assuming that he had years of talk therapy with a native guide in the hope all such patients have of arriving at an oasis of painlessness.

Because, of course, it isn't the ears. Or it isn't only the ear flaps. On the inside of one of them (left? right? does it matter?) he has a perforated drum and a 60% deficiency. He had a classmate in the fifth and sixth grades, Charles Downey (Downing? Dowland?) who had only one arm, the other never having developed or having been lost in an accident of some kind. Our awkward protagonist never had the nerve or poise to inquire, assuming that Charles would have been offended, which is not necessarily true. *(Dieu et mon gauche!)* Had it ever crossed his mind that such an inquiry could be an expression of concern rather than mere curiosity, he might have contrived a veil of friendship to make the question seem civil. But it didn't, and he knew what was in his mind and supposed that Charles would have had every right to take umbrage.

Hard of hearing, and also eczematous. It doesn't show anymore, but for most of his childhood he was afflicted, itched behind his knees and in the crook of his arm where his skin was broken out and scabby. And he was marked by that. Orthodox Jews don't allow people with skin diseases into the synagogue. The ancients couldn't tell the difference between eczema, psoriasis, rosacea, vitiligo, lichen planus, and leprosy, so, to be on the safe side, they declared them all 'unclean.' Our protagonist is by no means orthodox (although he is Jewish) but he agrees with the rabbis. Unclean. He didn't need the bell lepers used to have to ring as they walked along the roads to warn others away. Its tinkle was always with him. Shrinks would call it a wound to his self-image. But more fancifully we might say that he was a narcissist afraid of looking at the water.

SPEAKING OF SHRINKS, I was at a party once where I heard a distinguished psychiatrist opine (they tend to do that) that all intelligent children need psychotherapy. To cope with the loneliness. Cope? How, for God's sake? Make friends with kids who are less intelligent? (That works up to the third grade, maybe.) Learn to be lonely with the company of books and, now, electronic games? That's less fanciful but doesn't solve the problem. Come to understand that, as an ugly duckling, your prospects among the swans are good. But what kid can imagine the future? You're nine or ten, and you don't remember much before you were three. So your entire conscious lifetime is seven years maybe. You have no idea what a decade is, let alone a generation.

The most the therapist might aim for is to get the patient to understand that it isn't his fault, that it isn't the other kids' fault either, that there isn't even any fault involved. And not to take it personally. (How in hell do you contrive not to take your life personally? Are any of us capable of that? At any age?) These may be smart kids but they're not yet capable of such absurdist wisdom. And it's even more difficult for a bright kid who is also small, hard of hearing, and itchy.

WHY HASN'T THE STORY STARTED? I agree that this is outrageous. But it is difficult for a narrator to say much if his protagonist is reluctant. I can understand his disinclination to begin or, rather, to go back and relive painful moments in a life that have blurred over the decades so that only a few sharp (and dangerous) fragments remain. No, we should descend to the personal and liken these findings to a box of ancient photographs, some creased, some torn, some faded by exposure to the light, in which he can recognize some images but is unable to recover their contexts. (Yes, that's me in the field under the tree, but what field, what tree? We were visiting someplace in the country, a farm, maybe, or a place that had once been a farm but had become a mere residence out in the sticks. They had goats, I remember. But who were they? I can remember what they looked like but not their names. Who, for that matter, took the picture?)

The story? Yes, yes!

This unimpressive kid is torn between two girls (women, we'd say now, but back then girls). He was 'involved' as they put it politely then and now with both of them. Why two? Why not two? Girls with more than one sexual partner were promiscuous, but boys were boulevardiers, enviably louche figures from Peter Arno cartoons. But that's only part of the reason—assuming, that is, that there are reasons for anything.

Think of his social and sexual backwardness. For him to get a girl to go to bed with him and intentionally and even eagerly to have sex with him was amazing. Incredible, even after it had happened. With an itchy, deaf, dwarf like him? He needed confirmation. How to accomplish that persuasively except by going to bed with somebody else? I have no evidence for this idea, but it has a dim logic with which he doesn't argue. It makes sense that compulsive womanizers are men who cannot believe they are acceptable (let alone loveable) and keep searching to allay doubts they cannot otherwise conquer. After all, any woman who would settle for one of these men is unlikely to have standards high enough for him to take her opinion (and behavior) seriously. Nuts, of course, but many young and not so young men are. The women are badly used, maybe, but for their part the men aren't much better off. It isn't lust that drives Don Giovanni but rather a feeling of profound worthlessness to which he is a more abject servant than Leporello is to him.

But the don isn't quite the monster he appears to be. He's just an outlier on a wide spectrum. There's a little of him in each of us, and, when the opportunity presents itself (herself), it is difficult to resist. What we should realize in his shriek in the last act (hair-raising if it's done right) when he is descending into the torments of hell is that it's the shock of recognition as he—and we—realize that he has been living there all along.

You don't suppose our callow protagonist knows any of this, do you? (Has he even seen Don Giovanni?) He has never given serious thought to the meaning of his carrying on. (Carryings-on? There are two of them, remember.) One might even ask whether he has given any thought at all to anything in his sheltered and uneventful existence. Astonishingly, he has never had to make any choices more important than what to order in a restaurant, what shirt to buy in a haberdashery, or what courses to take in which the classes are not too early in the morning. He has never needed to and, in fact, hasn't been allowed to. Any deviations from his parents' plans for him would have been defiance, a 'betrayal' (they used that word a lot), and a display of ingratitude for their many sacrifices. It would have been a pointless and perverse behavior, hurtful to himself and ruinous to their far too specific dreams for him.

Unfair? That can't be a serious question. Unhealthy, say, because it was poisonous to everybody involved. At best, family life can have occasional moments of relative (just so!) tranquility. Most of the time for most people, it is an ongoing asymmetrical war, which is the nastiest kind. Most youngsters in college are therefore suffering from PTSD in one form or another, which may help explain why their behavior is so often erratic and irrational. Their youth and inexperience also contribute. Nevertheless, the folkways require these children to make sound decisions about what they want to do with their lives and with whom they want to spend them. We Westerners look at arranged marriages, for instance, with some disdain, but they are less chancy, and kinder, because they do not raise unlikely hopes of a passion that will last forever.

They've read novels, these kids. The books were assigned with their nonsensical endorsements of love and marriage that were seconded by their English teachers. (Mostly they believe what teachers tell them. About algebra and geometry, surely, and to a slightly lesser extent other subjects, too.) Then, after school, they watch television shows, see movies, and hear pop songs that drum (literally) the same thing into their heads in simpler and more explicit terms. This is all too talky, I am afraid, but it is important that you understand how the protagonist was not just empty-headed. Worse, his head had been filled for years with dangerous misinformation.

We can skip the clunky machinery of how he met Leah (at a freshman mixer, maybe?), how he later on he met Jennifer (he has absolutely no idea), and how he then found himself in a dream existence with both girls at the same time, which he does remember and took to be utter bliss. For one thing, the conventions of romantic comedy have exhausted our interest in these encounters. For another, the poor author is himself unable to contribute any useful details about them. He remembers what Leah looked like, because he married her and lived with her for twenty years. And there were pictures around the house of her at this age or only a little older. Jenny he can barely recall. A long, graceful neck and a cleanly chiseled Avedon-like chin above which there was a softness to her face that is, sixty years later, still appealing even if hopelessly blurred. And great legs, of the kind one would see on a Greek Venus, if perhaps a little less heavy in the thighs. But that's too high-flown. Say it's a spring day and for the first time coats are gone and, as in Irwin Shaw's splendid title, there are the 'Girls in their Summer Dresses.' A breeze ruffles a skirt here and there –not exaggeratedly as in 'Seven Year Itch' with Marilyn, but just a little. Maybe once in twenty times, once in fifty times, he will think *yes* and only moments later realize that what he has affirmed is the similarity of those legs to Jenny's. And then there is a slight (still!) pang. What else? Her elocution was impressive and her voice was low in pitch, a contralto that gave whatever she said a seriousness. Or sometimes a sexiness. She has, we must admit, an unfair advantage over Leah. Having faded into a barely visible, barely audible wraith, an idea of an idea, she is necessarily flawless. She couldn't have been, but the passage of time has promoted her. Usually time tarnishes love affairs, bringing them down from the heights of fantasy and lust to the quotidian dreariness of fondness, compatibility and friendliness. But that never happened with him and Jenny. Their love never dwindled; it was just interrupted, so that he looked back on its frozen memory in anguish. It had been incomparable. There are still apotheoses, less spectacular than they used to be, perhaps, but of an effect every bit as astonishing.

I get ahead of myself. We return to his dream state of that three or four months. Happiness, not just multiplied by two but squared. For the first time in his life, he feels good about himself. Each of them is attractive, intelligent, sophisticated (more than he is, certainly). And each of them loves him. It is beyond imagining. But that is the essence of the problem. Had he been able to imagine it accurately and realistically, he'd have been able to project a little and understand that this was an inherently unstable arrangement to which there was a degree of risk—to both of them and to him, too. To him, first, because he was at that point a self-centered little creature. Or as self-centered as a kid without much sense of self can be.

LET'S BE HONEST WITH ONE ANOTHER. You can see what's coming as well as I. We're not so dim as he seems to have been. We have read stories like this before, and something always happens to disturb the precarious equilibrium of the lovers' lives. (Otherwise, they wouldn't be stories, would they?) All the books, movies, and newspaper accounts agree. There must be a come-uppance, preferably catastrophic and spectacular. Murder, suicide, or, back in the day, retirement to a nunnery or monastery. Doesn't our callow fellow realize this? Hasn't he read anything? I said he was a smart kid, but where is that smartness?

Perversely, the intelligence is what's wrong. He's clever enough to realize that it would only be the unhappy endings that present themselves in fiction. For one thing, that's the tradition. But for another, what would be the point in writing about a guy who is carrying on simultaneously with two different women and, either by luck or shrewdness, manages to keep both affairs going for years? (An interesting idea but who would believe it?) All you'd need is meticulousness. Spies manage to maintain two (or more) different lives, and they aren't all discovered and killed. Look beyond the fictions then, and try to imagine what the real world is like. It's anyone's guess. Bright children assume that grownups know what they're doing and understand what life is like but conspire with one another to hide all useful information from them (by switching to Yiddish for instance). But there are no secrets. Later on, the one thing professors can't say in class is that they don't know anything either. That nobody knows anything. That we are all in Plato's cave.

I am talking generally here, because I can't speak for the author or ask him. He wouldn't remember anyway what he was thinking all those decades ago. The likelihood is that he was too pleased with himself, too entranced by the wonderful memories of last weekend and how they merged with the fine prospects of the coming one, to think at all. Or even to breathe. Trying to keep up with his schoolwork, maybe he was too busy. Not that it matters much. Thinking would not have done him any good. The sad truth is that the thoughtful analysis only began years later when it was retrospective and otiose. The only use to it has been as a means of self-flagellation: the clearer his understanding gets, the sharper are the claws—which are what the thongs of a cat o'nine tails are called. (Really? Really. I Googled it. And one of the sites to which they referred me was Amazon, which sells cats o'nine tails—if that's the plural—quite reasonably.)

YES, I'M WASTING TIME. I'm sorry. But it is a painful prospect we face, and if the doctor is a little late for a spinal puncture, what patient is going to complain? But before the crucial moment, let us amuse ourselves a bit more by enjoying his...couple of months? Three? He will tell you that it was the happiest time of his life and he can't even remember how long it lasted. What sense does that make? After all those years of waiting and enduring, of being mocked for his intelligence ('walking dictionary' or, more painful because there was a grain of truth in it, 'show-off'), he now has two beautiful, intelligent, sexy twenty-year-old women with a quick sense of humor and a sufficient fund of general information so that he doesn't have to explain any reference more obscure than Santa Claus and Mickey Mouse. They both love him. Better yet, they appreciate him. Admire him, even. And through them, he can begin to tolerate himself, entertaining for the first time the possibility that he is not a total yutz. He realizes this and understands that he is using them, but if anyone were to accuse him of this, he would reply, correctly I think, that we all use one another all the time and in all aspects of relationships, including the physical.

Unconditional love? If that's what you want, buy a dog. What connoisseurs prefer is the love that comes from a discriminating evaluation of their minds and looks, and maybe how well they dress. And dance. Earned love! Isn't that what each of us thinks he has and has deserved (although most of us are wrong)?

OR, NO, HE TELLS ME it was more than a couple of months. Maybe half a year. Maybe even a little more. He remembers that he and Jenny spent time together during the summer between his junior and senior years. He was granted another of those images that arise occasionally from the mental murk and he can see the two of them holding hands and walking out together onto the Tappan Zee Bridge. Only there wasn't any bridge, yet. Just the structure on pilings that would connect to the bridge when it was floated downriver.

This meant that there was one of those surrealist highways that movie directors love, a six-lane road that left the Nyack shore, jutted out over the water, and came to an abrupt stop. Suddenly, nothing but thin air and, down below, water.

(And down below that, mud, which is inherently unstable. The reason the Tappan Zee was built there was to keep the project upriver from where the Port Authority of New York—and the Democrats— would control it and could hire the contractors. Above that line where the bridge is, it was Governor Malcolm Wilson and the Albany Republicans who would manage the project and hand out the enormously lucrative contracts. That it was the worst place in the river to put a bridge didn't matter. Nobody uses the name, but it is actually 'The Governor Malcolm Wilson Tappan Zee Bridge,' so that his cupidity and stupidity are memorialized by a 1,212-foot-long monstrosity that is already falling apart and will have to be closed in 2107.

The author knows all this because of his sentimental attachment if not to the cantilever bridge in the middle then to that west side approachway. Which is, in Latin, a *pons sublicius*, a bridge resting on piles. (It is amazing how seldom that word from Caesar's *Gallic Wars* comes up in adult life.)

He remembers the gloriousness of walking out there with Jenny, the sun on her face, and the wind in her hair, fluffing it for a moment, then subsiding, and coming back to toy with it again. And her lovely peals of laughter he has remembered every time he has driven across the bridge. How could he have forgotten that summer? To avoid the truth of its reprimand? It is only our conversations that have prompted its somewhat belated reappearance. I wait to hear more, but he says nothing. Distress? Or because there isn't any more that he can recall, which would be yet another reason for his unhappiness. Whatever it is, I do not press him. I am his narrator, not his therapist, after all. (And, no, they are not the same thing.)

It wasn't an obsession. For years he didn't give much thought to her and that other life he would have had with her. But even during those periods of remission, traversing the Tappan Zee would produce a reliable twinge, which he welcomed. Those who have been bereaved cling to their moments of sudden grief because they are the last connections with the deceased. In that same way, he welcomed that frisson of shame and its reassurance that his life was not wholly discontinuous. In some way the young man he had once been had not entirely disappeared. Nor had she. That thought enlivened his drive, at least for the few minutes until he reached the entrance to the Garden State Parkway.

Is this how one measures love? Is there any better or other way? Pindar's great trick was to rise from quotidian to the mythic and then, gracefully, gently, descend again to what is the world we know and believe in. So you mustn't blame him too much or me. There is precedent to which we can appeal.

What a complicated explanation for a simple & direct phenomenon! The abruptness of the emotion, its bitterness and, simultaneously, the rueful pleasure arising from it require some fastidious untangling. If I inquire too bluntly, he clams up angrily and sulks. And we—you, the reader, and I—come to an awkward standstill.

PLEASURE? Yes, because next to him, more times than not, Leah was sitting on the passenger side, listening to music on the radio, and looking idly out of the window. She hadn't the faintest idea that he had been, however briefly, with Jenny again. It had lasted only milliseconds, but physicists base their complicated theories on events that are infinitely briefer. If it's real, how long it lasts isn't important. 'It has been' still applies, for the rest of eternity. That can be a curse or a blessing, but either way past is persistent, however much we may try to evade it.

So where were we? Or they? On their uncompleted bridge. It is only with the greatest restraint that I refuse the tempting metaphor offered by those six lanes of concrete road that connected to nothing but just stopped. A figuration of the lovers' prospects? Too obvious, even if our protagonist might like it. His tastes and mine do not necessarily coincide, and I am not always obliged to yield to him on these matters even if it is his damned book and he is real while I am a mere figment. He has an existence in the real world while I live only in these pages. In the far distance is . . . Tarrytown. And some industrial facility belonging, he thinks, to General Motors. Very large but unimpressive. It occurs to me that if the bridge hadn't yet been completed, he must have had to take the ferry that used to run back and forth between Tarrytown and Nyack. But of those pleasant river crossings he recalls nothing. On the way over he was no doubt anticipating and on the way back, savoring and remembering, so it is hard to chide him for his inattention. If anything, his inability to recall details of the ride does him some credit.

What made those halcyon days possible was Leah's summer in Europe on an academic (more or less) program that took her to Florence. This meant that there were no tactical constraints to his meetings with Jenny. He had a summer job (partly for the money, of course, but also because his parents thought it was good for his character). He worked in the pantry of a mental hospital, delivering fruits and vegetables to the various cottages on the grounds of the New York

Hospital Westchester Division. Bloomingdale's was how people referred to it, because it was on Bloomingdale Road. (There's an actual Bloomingdale's there now, the store I mean, which seems pleonastic.) He had a little cart to wheel through the tunnels that connected the different buildings. He filled the orders in the morning. Seven apples for Ward H—but they all had to be the same size, because if one was a little larger the loonies might fight about it. Or if one had a bird peck, they might fight about that. And then he'd take off on his route that was just under a mile in those damp, spooky tunnels. It wasn't strenuous. And the pay wasn't bad for a summer job for a college kid. But it confirmed in some small way his notions about 'work' and being a 'grown-up,' in that nobody seemed to notice the silliness of what they were doing. There were a couple of grown men with him in the supply room (Teddy and another whose name he cannot generate) and they instructed him about the importance of having all the apples just the same with perfectly straight faces.

Most weekends, he would cross the river on Fridays to be with Jenny until Sunday afternoon. That her mother didn't object was wonderful. That his own parents didn't object either was miraculous. It ever dawned on him until much later that their reasoning (if you want to call it that) was that this couldn't be serious because the girl wasn't Jewish. Wild oats. Or wild kasha. Had she been a member of the tribe, they would have worried that he was tying himself down too early, wasn't ready for a committed relationship, and should 'play the field.' This, they thought, was safe, or at least safer.

Bigotry? Yes, surely. But what could he do? He couldn't discipline them. Or lecture to them. He couldn't disown them—to be realistic about it, he needed them to continue to pay his tuition and room-and-board costs. He was grateful to them for having worked so hard to lavish on him the best education the country offers. And anyway, the freedom he enjoyed, for whatever unacceptable reason, was welcome. If there was going to be a fight, the later the better. Sufficient unto the day is the evil thereof. (Matthew, maybe? But it sounds Epicurean.) Was this cowardice? Diplomacy? Prudence? All those together, surely. He has regrets, but not about that radiant summer and his having benefited from their distorted views about what was permissible for him.

To be fair about it, though (Why?)(Why not?), it was only ten years or so after the Shoah. Jews were like great grey owls or pine martens or thought they were, on the endangered species list, the herd having been recently thinned by six million. Our protagonist, or, more likely, his parents could have found any number of non-insane rabbis who would have stroked their beards and suggested that they were correct. Intermarriage imperils the race. (Is it a race?) And intermarriage with a shiksa (a female non-Jew) was worse than the other way because Jewish identity is matrilineal. A Jewish girl marries a shegetz (a male non-Jew) and their children are Jewish. With a Jewish mother, a child is Jewish, whether the father is a wonder rabbi or a Cossack rapist. With a shiksa, the children would have to be converted, assuming that the woman were willing to allow that. And it still wouldn't be a Jewish home, would it? (Not that it has anything to do with this, but in Salt Lake City, if you're not a Mormon, you're a gentile, even if you're a Jew.)

I don't care about any of this, nor did our love-struck young man. But it wasn't just the thought but the words themselves that betray the fear and animosity. *Shiksa* and *shegetz* come from the root of a word that means 'detestable,' so they are hardly morally neutral, even if the rest of the ideas about these things are defensible. American Jews who have only a few words of Yiddish don't realize the unpleasantness of these words and use them without ill intent. (*Goy*, however, simply means 'nation' and although it is generally applied to other nations, it carries with it no inherent disesteem—beyond whatever otherness implies. Jews are a people among peoples, a religion among religions—Moslems, Catholics, Primitive Baptists, Mormons, Druzes or any other agglomeration of superstition-sharers you can offer.)

Which leaves us with the parents being bigots although not quite rabid about it. For them and for the son, too it was an uncomfortable place to be. It would have been tough for him to argue the point with a lawyer (which his father happened to be) who didn't care about being right but, as with so many of his colleagues at the bar, about winning. And here he had some arguments, however odd to which he could appeal (at the top of his voice, no doubt).

And she? Jenny's mother? He has no idea and neither do I. His guess would be that whatever she may have felt, she had the good manners and political liberalism not to let it show—even to herself, maybe. She was always gracious to him, charming, friendly. Enlightened, too, because I'm sure she understood that Jenny and her visitor were screwing their brains out at every opportunity. But Jenny had been fitted for a diaphragm and was a healthy young woman. Had it come to a question of marriage, she might have hesitated, on the grounds of incompatibility (a tactful way of saying Jewishness). But he doubts it. In any event, they never got that far.

Doubts? Guesses? Are they enough? In novels, they are as good as certainties. 'I think therefore I am,' Descartes declares. No novelist of any seriousness would go much farther than to say, 'I think I think, and therefore I think I am.'

IT'S POSSIBLE THAT I AM WRONG and that, whatever she thought, Jenny's mother was clever enough to let her daughter make her own mistakes. Why get excited about a sophomore's love affair? The odds against it lasting were good. And often the best thing for a parent to do is nothing. It avoids corrosive arguments and future resentments. Time may not be a reliable healer but with time this kind of problem can solve itself. Our author can't be sure because he didn't know her well enough. How could he have? She was a woman of impressive sophistication and he could not have been expected to understand her worldliness. As he realized at the time.

In the end, it made no difference. It wasn't her mother or even his parents who destroyed his and Jenny's prospects. He did this himself. Him. No one else is to blame. He should have been braver or smarter. He should have behaved better. Or, no, we all want to behave better. But say more modestly that he could have behaved differently, and that is sufficient for him to feel the shame that is with him always, like an arthritic joint that in certain weather sends its familiar signals of distress.

This is an instance in which my participation is helpful. His recollection is blurred by sorrow and guilt and also by the idealization we accord the dead. (Yes, she's dead.) I can come in and declare as fact what I can only infer from his hints and, more often, prolonged silences. If I make guesses that he doesn't correct, I assume that I've discovered some truth or other. We have it that she was pretty, or maybe went beyond prettiness to a minor kind of beauty. (More than that tends to corrupt the character of many young women.) She was sexually enthusiastic. But this is not much more detailed than one of Trollope's descriptions, is it? What must be added is her wit, her playfulness, and her gift for gentle or not-so-gentle mockery (and self-mockery). Now and again, she used to say 'crapola,' which he understood instantly as a relic from childhood. Long since cleansed of any scatological reference, it was the expression of an outraged eleven-year-old (more or less) attempting to swear but with no adequate repertoire of naughty words. This one she almost certainly picked up on the playground. (One can't imagine her mother saying such a thing.) And for her to revert to the locution at nineteen or twenty would have been the equivalent of holding on to a bedraggled Teddy bear. Or flinging it against a wall in frustration, the way she might have done a decade earlier. What mattered was that she could rely on him to hear it and comprehend instantly its various levels of meaning. Which he did, as, simultaneously, he felt a delight in how she had trusted in him to do it.

They talked. They talked voluminously, often about poetry because he liked it and had committed a fair amount to memory. His odd view, then and now, is that one does better just finding a poem and reading it oneself than having it assigned by a teacher. She thought at first that he was being contrarian and perverse but she came to understand what he meant and how he considered the encounter with a poem to be an intimate transaction. He read poems to her, and that was intimate too. She liked funny poems or, say, poems with wit in them, and her occasional chuckle—or amused snort—was proof that she was getting them, the poem, the poet, and him, too. (Snort is wrong. It was between a snort and a sniff, a sign that she was amused but also amused by her being amused at that ridiculous, crapola joke.)

What else he can remember? The insubstantiality of shades in Hades is not their doing: it is what happens in the memories of the survivors who loved them and are trying to bring back details that are increasingly difficult to recover. We attribute our own imprecision to them and imagine them as semi-transparent, gauzy beings, beckoning phantoms that disintegrate even as we reach toward them.

She drank her coffee black. No sugar. Nothing. He thought this was sophisticated of her. In movies, tough guys drank black coffee. It was probably a practice she had learned from her mother or her (deceased) father, but her explanation was that if the coffee was any good, it shouldn't be mucked around with. And this was in the fifties before the drink became a fetish. He took it with a little milk and sugar, which she disapproved of but tolerated. She said if he tried it her way for a while, he'd get used to it and even come to like it. He did and drinks it black even now although he still likes a non-calorie sweetener in it but with each cup, as he tears the little blue packet open, he admits that this is a defect in his character.

Does this get us any closer to their relationship? Do we see them more clearly? I despair of finding ways to convey what it was like for these youngsters who were supremely happy together. Happiness is difficult to describe, maybe because we are less introspective when we are in that rare but delightful state. Why mess with it? Misery loves to analyze itself, figure out reasons (assuming that there are reasons), and perhaps make plans to improve. Happiness doesn't want to change and doesn't have to do anything.

This kind of conundrum may have been what drove Alain Robbe-Grillet and Marguerite Duras to the *nouveau romain,* in which, ideally, there were no characters at all, just objects. Furniture, bric-a-brac, stuff that may not mean much but doesn't mislead or lie. And you never have to tell furniture to shut the fuck up. That kind of writing has a theoretical purity but the air at that altitude is too thin to breathe.

WE ALL REMEMBER the dreary schoolroom exercise: compare and contrast. With our protagonist, there was the possibility of doing that, which became, after a time, almost inescapable. He'd met Leah first. She was the first girl with whom he had had sexual intercourse, which is a significant moment in a young man's life. (More than in young women's lives? Conceivably.) It hadn't been her first time though. Either then or soon thereafter, she told him about her deflowering in the backseat of a car in the Watchung Mountains and she named the guy. (He still remembers the name, although he wouldn't confide it to me.) To challenge him? To see how possessive he might be? To whet even further the sharp edge of his desire? To boast? All these years later he hasn't figured it out , although he has thought about it now and then. His persistent inability to answer that question raises a further and more fundamental one about whether anyone can ever know what someone else is thinking? Words? They invite misuse and often tell us nothing more than the speaker's intention—which is often to mislead. The truth, as Wilde remarked, is rarely pure and never simple. What he could have added is that it is almost always private.

IT COULDN'T HAVE BEEN AN INADVERTENT letting down of
her guard, though, for when she got back from Florence and schools
resumed (hers, Jenny's, and his), she informed him, fairly casu-
ally, that she had had 'a relationship' in Florence. Not with one of
those seductive Italians who prey on American students, but with an
Australian. (What was he to make of the fact that he was an Aussie?
That this wasn't the usual and banal screwing a local but had some
originality to it? That it was more sincere than it would have been
with a Florentine?)

He was...jealous, of course. But also relieved. If she could stray,
then so could he. It was impliedly a retroactive permission. Neither
of them had actually been unfaithful because there had never been
any explicit pledge of fidelity on either side. If he had assumed something different, that was his fault. Clearly, she had made no such
assumption or commitment, and, as he saw it, the way was now clear
for him to continue, shuttling back and forth to see each of them on
alternate weekends and maintain this fortunate arrangement for as
long as possible.

This is not to suggest that he was grateful to Leah for this license.
He regretted that she had been.... Thoughtless? (That would have
been the most generous interpretation.) He couldn't blame her
for screwing the Aussie over there, because he had behaved in the
same way here with Jenny. But at least he had had the courtesy not
to mention it. What possible reason could there be to burden her
with this knowledge? To obtain her pardon? But why risk hurting
her? These are difficult questions made all the more complicated by
the differences in temperament not only between men and wom-
en, but among men and among women. There are no models in
literature to which any of us can turn for philosophical counsel or
useful hints about strategy. The great novels of the nineteenth century were written, not at all surprisingly, in the nineteenth century.
Attitudes were different then. Nobody has an affair these days with a
married woman who, after a while, throws herself under a train (the

Metro North?). Operas, inherently extravagant and melodramatic, are worse, , With the sopranos bleeding to death but singing their hearts out, they seem to be about life on some other planet. Ahh! La Maledizione! (With the agonized high B!)

It would have almost certainly been in bed in a room at the Lincoln Hotel that she imparted this information to him. Oddly, that must have been the hotel that Dick Sassoon (a distant relative of Siegfried's) used to take Sylvia Plath when she came down from Northampton to visit. Where else could they have gone? She was an athletic fuck-er-around, and she told him about it, either then or a few years later when he went to meet her in Paris where they planned to get married. (All of this, her biographers tell us, is dismayingly true.) She told him about Hughes, who wasn't just another hunk football player but a real (although not very nice) person. She must have imparted this in-formation on the telephone, because by the time she got to Paris, he had fled to Madrid, breaking her heart—or so the books report.

Why did she tell him? Why did Leah tell me? The walls between the rooms at the Lincoln were thin, but not that thin. Plath, of course, was crazy. Leah was sane but complicated. Maybe it comes down to the simple fact that they were young and didn't know any better. Nobody knew anything. And for him here was no one to whom he could he turn for advice. His father? Not back then and certainly not that father. A teacher with whom he was friendly? That too would have been unthinkable in the fifties. A friendly classmate? He had heard stories of some of their adventures, most of which were less complicated and more unfortunate than his own and often involved expensive arrangements for abortions that were then illegal. Their disasters did not encourage confidence in their judgment and his knowledge of their trials and embarrassments in no way diminished the awkwardness he felt about discussing his predicament. (When did it become a predicament?) He knew, at some level, that what he was doing was wrong, delightful but also deceitful, a series of mis-representations that, if only implicit, were dishonest and shameful.

He liked both these girls. He admired them. He loved them. He loved their love. He could even claim that love had forced him to these falsehoods, however absurd that would be. The alternative, however, was to give one of them up. But which? Falsehood is an unpleasant word, but he was being false to both of them. Duplicitous? That could have been coined specifically with him in mind. Like most of us, he had to learn as he went along, and if God was dead and there were no persuasive morals, what could he rely on but instinct and... taste? But that, he was surprised to discover, was not a license for debauchery. He loved their flesh but that did not blind him to the fact that they were both people, individuals, lovable and worthy of fair dealing and respect. He took it as a fundamental principal that they were to be kept separate: it would have been disgraceful, for instance, to try to arrange to have sex with each of them on the same day. It never even occurred to him to try to discover some novel maneuver or position or gesture with one and then introduce it to the other the following weekend. It was not an athletic event and he was not, he told himself, an absolute pig, even as he wondered whether pigs, if they could think, might not disapprove of his behavior. (No, but swans would and, among mammals, wolves, beavers, and—no joke! —Malagasy jumping rats.)

To compare them in any way would have seemed calculating and unattractive. And he was convinced that it would be a useless exercise. What his emotions told him had little to do with mere data. There were times, though, when he couldn't help observing differences between them. He and Jenny were in bed one night in that New Haven hotel and they both happened to be awake. In an attempt (mostly) to achieve an even greater intimacy and to get to know her better, he asked her, thinking of Leah, how she had lost her virginity. She laughed and asked why he wanted to know.

'I don't know. Just curious. Or, no, it's supposed to be a big thing, and it's part of your life. That's why.'

She said it hadn't been such a big thing. 'It was like getting my ears pierced. I thought it was time, you know?'

She had had a summer internship in a museum, and there had been a curator there, one of the few straight ones, and he was nice enough and good looking enough. And he was married, which had been one of her requirements, because she didn't want to start anything serious. She waited until the end of the summer and then, the last week, went to bed with him. It wasn't terrible, she said, but it wasn't all that wonderful either.

He asked her how she had managed to get him to do this.

'You've got to be kidding. It isn't even a matter of sending out *yes* signals. All you have to do—all I have to do, anyway—is to stop sending out negative ones. It's like scattering breadcrumbs in the park. The birds come.'

She was funny and candid and was telling him only because he had asked. She had been relaxed about it and...amusing. He couldn't help thinking how Leah had been aggressive, testing him to see whether he was grown-up enough to take it. Or for some other reason he'd never managed to figure out. But it hadn't been friendly. There he was, comparing them, but he couldn't help it.

What he decided, if it can be called a decision, was to do nothing, to wait and see what would happen. To meddle now would surely be to ruin a dream that had contrived to realize itself for him. Even though he was living it, checking bus and train schedules, borrowing cars from classmates, and managing to get his reading done and his papers written, he couldn't quite believe it. If this was life, then everything else in his experience or even his imagination was dull and irrelevant. Only this was real. It was too splendid not to be.

WHAT OUR PROTAGONIST WOULD LIKE is for the book to end here. Why not? All those minatory novels start out on a high note, have some fun that readers can share, and then, as we are enjoying ourselves, nudge the hero and the heroine onto a path that declines inexorably to disaster. But why cooperate with the obsolete prejudices of novelists, their audiences, and their times? If you get to page 182, say, of *Anna Karenina* and just stop, you have an altogether different and much more cheerful book. Alternatively, we could put our young man in a car, have it crash on the tricky road over Pawling Mountain, and kill him off. An abrupt but paradoxically happy ending. He nods his head and acknowledges that that would have been satisfactory.

Characters have little to say about the plots of their lives. In books or in the world, we are the authors' manipulable toys whom they push this way and that to watch how we behave, but no one pays attention or is willing to learn from these demonstrations.

Believe me when I say that I have argued as well as I could for mercy for our inadequate protagonist. I have asked for compassion! He's way out of his depth. Only a kid, you remember, he is ill-equipped for making consequential choices in his life and the lives of others. He may have mastered simultaneous equations, but simultaneous girls are a more difficult problem. And the penalties for wrong answers are more serious than anyone that young can imagine.

The author, unmoved, shakes his head, refusing any temptation to be decent, much as God must refuse a thousand times a minute, not even amused anymore by earnest prayers for merciful exceptions but by now apparently just bored. The protagonist is also stubborn and unable to forgive himself, so that my plea is ineffective.

It wasn't long after Leah came back from Florence that she heard about his involvement with Jenny. They were in different colleges but that wasn't as much a buffer as he had assumed. Each had friends who had friends. The seven sister colleges were thus a loosely connected, extended community. There was every likelihood that somebody at one place might know someone at the other. All that was needed to bridge these few degrees of separation was some casual reference that surprised an acquaintance enough to remark about it to another friend. Gossip. Females do that. Put two women together, total strangers, in some accidental conjunction, at the hairdresser's perhaps, and within an hour each knows how many children the other has and their ages and genders, and her marital status. Not infrequently they exchange medical histories, too, although I can't imagine why. All that information gets transmitted like viruses through the air they are both breathing.

Leah could have telephoned him. But she decided (I am assuming) that it would be better to confront him face-to-face and study his expression while he was saying whatever he was going to say. Unfair? So much the better. Giving her a little credit, which is better for our understanding of these events—she wasn't stupid after all— she might have preferred a live interview because it was a likelier way to get at the truth. (Is there such a thing?) She had for whatever reason confessed her adventure with the Australian. Had he taken that information as a license for his own behavior? If that was his claim, she was prepared with a riposte with which she was eager to surprise him: 'He's in Australia. And it's over. With you, she is here and it's going on now. For Christ's sake, surely, you can see the difference!'

Could he? Can we? He might have argued that she was appealing to some unwritten rule she had just made up and that he couldn't have known about. That is, of course, *l'esprit de l'escalier,* or would be if there weren't some limit to the length of the *escalier* and the pause before the smart reply. Sixty-some-odd years later, he can at last come up with a reasonable response. But then? Not only did he not know what he was doing; he didn't even have any idea how to talk about it, lacking not only the vocabulary but the poise.

He did manage to ask her what then was the point of her telling him about her Australian? To boast? To see how much he would tolerate without complaining? Or just to hurt him? Not that succinctly, of course. It took him much phumphering around but he managed eventually to make himself clear.

41

'Oh, no,' she answered, 'you can't turn this around and attack me! You're the one in the wrong.' A long venomous pause, with her eyelids narrowed but not blinking. He thought she looked in that instant like a viper about to strike and...and was enjoying herself. He couldn't think of anything to say.

'Think about it,' she said quietly. And to give him time to do that, she departed, less than an hour after having arrived, to take a train to New York and leave him alone with his (presumably guilty) thoughts.

THAT'S MOSTLY INVENTED. He isn't exactly an idiot, but he can't remember even the most vital moments of his life. He has no idea where they were. His room? A restaurant? A bench in some courtyard or on the green? Or exactly what happened or when. He is ashamed of himself, but that doesn't jog his memory. There are only wisps of the will, tiny details he can recover after long, trance-like thought. Specifics about either one of them fade away. He was married to Leah for almost twenty years, but she is already like a fresco in a damp, rural church from which the paint has been gradually peeling. The little village can't afford to have it restored and the artist was not important enough for the government to get involved. So the mural—an annunciation, let us suppose—continues in its steady deterioration. There are even theoreticians who object to any meddling. This is the object and it has its life. Does anyone want to put the arms back on the Venus de Milo?

That's what the foregoing scene is, though, a restoration, an imagined moment in a popularizing biography. (He must have thought.... She might have answered....) It's fine if you don't care about the truth. Even in novels, these enlivening details are distracting inventions. They are like the pieces of gravel birds swallow to help grind up whatever they've eaten, useful perhaps but not, in themselves, nutritious. Consider your recollection of a novel, even a great one that you read ten or twenty years ago. What details do you remember? What was Becky Sharp wearing on her way to Amelia's house

42

in Russell Square? What color was the horse Squire Allworthy gave Tom Jones? The novelist may have hesitated for an instant before he decided on something and then, dipping his pen in the inkwell, continued with the sentence. What stays with us for years is the mood of the book, its ruefulness or ridiculousness or wit. And the texture of its prose, maybe. And beyond those things, in a very few, very great books there is a kind of wisdom.

But to return from this depressing divagation, let me assert baldly that she said something, whatever it was and however it was delivered. It would have been in the fall, probably. But anything beyond that is only speculation on the author's part or mine. What it amounted to, of course, was what he ought to have been expecting sooner or later from of one of the young women or the other: her or me. Decide.

Lie? That was certainly a possibility. It is what he would recommend now to that long-gone lad. Say something diplomatic to put the unpleasantness off for a few more weeks or months. (That's just another way of describing lies.) Pronounce whatever phrases are necessary to restore the status quo. But that wouldn't have resolved anything. And however unwittingly he had fallen into this situation, he now had to recognize that to lie—to either of them or both—would only make things worse, which was not something he wanted to do. Morally wrong? That's very lofty. Certainly it was unattractive, which was something he could grasp. It was dissonant with his still primitive ideas of who he was and how he should conduct himself.

So what to do? Her? Or her? He loved both of them, although in different ways. As Biblical Jews understood perfectly well, a love for one woman doesn't blind a man to the appeal of another. Back then, to have but one wife was to be poor. Adultery was forbidden but polygamy was perfectly okay.

Could he deny the truth of his own experience? Leah's adventure in Florence was relevant (although he was not to discover its meaning for years). That they had had problems didn't bother him as much as it should have. It never crossed his mind to project forward and imagine how these restive assertions of hers of independence might manifest themselves over the decades in a marriage. For that matter, her declaration of this ultimatum was, given her history, peremptory and unfair. She had confessed to—boasted of—two sexual liaisons. That he knew about. Wasn't he entitled to just one?

But this mischaracterizes his thinking, which may have been roughly along those lines but was more politely muddled. What ideas could he entertain that weren't calculating and, to that degree, offensive? Is this what love is supposed to do? (And who is doing the supposing?) It isn't a joke (although of course it is) that sociologists define love as a condition in which rewards exceed costs by a margin greater than what is readily available in the vicinity. It is almost courageous of them to reduce so grand a mystery to so blunt an economic calculation, because it is offensive to our sensibilities. But that doesn't mean it isn't true. This was the kind of cerebration he now found himself forced into, and he found it distasteful. Lists of pros and cons? Did Tristan do this with Isolde, or Antony with Cleopatra? It's not a wisecrack. The sad fact is that all these courses in literature, music, art, philosophy, and history fail to tell the students a damned thing about how to live, and think, and be. For all their reading, lectures, seminars, and papers, they find themselves reduced to the condition of illiterate bumpkins. (The bumpkins, in fact, have an advantage because they have fewer misleading illusions.)

Du Côté de chez Jenny, the ledger was that of a treasure house. A bright, beautiful, funny, sexy, and kind person. All he could want. On the minus side, there was only the one thing—the fact that she wasn't Jewish. And he didn't care, about that, not in the least. It wasn't even a religious question—she was a Unitarian and he, a non-practicing Jew—but purely racial. His parents were not devout. They had a Seder every year and went to services on High Holidays but otherwise took no particular notice of Jewish culture or customs or commandments. They didn't keep kosher and ate bacon and lobster—as well as pastrami and corned beef and bagels and lox from Gordon's Delicatessen. The expression of their religion that had made the greatest impression on him had been a negative— their refusal to have a Christmas tree. Otherwise, their religiosity was confined to a few odd superstitions: he was never allowed to go around the house in stockinged feet, for instance, because that was what one did when mourning, so it would be the equivalent of wishing them dead. And to marry outside the tribe, they believed, would be like marrying outside the species. A shiksa? Absolutely not! Over our dead bodies! No, they wouldn't kill themselves, but it was not unimaginable that they would disown him, treat him as if he were dead, and even take off their shoes and sit *shiva* for him.

He knew these things and did not know them. If someone had asked him, he might have found his way to a more or less accurate response, but he was able to repress, deny, and avoid, as most of us can in painful situations. His behavior, however, would not have been different even if he had been conscious of the shiksa problem. He always went to visit her across the river, but the ferry ran both ways and he had never asked her to cross from Rockland to Westchester to spend a weekend with his family. It never occurred to him. She was innately tactful and never asked. Anyway, his great preference was to spend time with her and her family. Her mother was charming. He could make her younger sister Marcia laugh. There was more room (although the houses were pretty much the same size). She was only a freshman, so any idea of an engagement and the necessary introduction of Jenny to his family was far in the hazy future.

Had he thought about it, he could have figured out the reason for his parents' permissiveness. As long at the girl was just a name to them, she remained theoretical: they could tell themselves, although not perhaps aloud, that until they were introduced to her they could suppose it wasn't serious. Let him go across the river and do whatever he was doing.

For his part, he could not argue about what had not yet been actually said. He didn't have to do the calculations or work out the practical consequences, because he knew perfectly well that they would explode and that, if he held his ground, there would be a complete rupture. He would have to make his own way in the world. He would have to find the money to pay his spring term tuition. Or, no, he would have to drop out of school and get a job.

He tried to imagine it. He even took some comfort in the idea that Jenny would wait for him. He could go to New York, find something to do to feed himself, and keep going. He supposed he could eventually go back to school at night and get his degree (not so prestigious as the one he would get if he stayed where he was, but a respectable one). It would not be the end of the world. All he needed besides his love for her was faith in himself (more than he had) and courage (more than he had). These deficiencies were grim things to have to admit.

Oddly, they weighed in Jenny's favor. She was the choice he knew he would make if he were a better person and had the nerve. Leah's was the easy, cowardly way. And he had an odd premonition that, shrewd as she was, she would sooner or later realize this—if not in months then years hence. Her mind worked in ways that he could hardly understand, and he already had the impression that she was not at all grateful for his having overlooked her sexual adventures. Contemptuous, even? He couldn't rule that out. If he were to marry her, she would someday realize what he had done and why and would—justifiably—despise him for it. Could he keep a secret like this from her for a lifetime? He was not confident in his discretion, either.

What if he said no to her? That would end their relationship (probably, but not even that was certain). Then he would be free to continue to see Jenny, an excellent solution, desirable in every way but one: his admission to himself that he might not, in the end, have the nerve to marry her was a defect of which he had not been previously aware but he was now and it bothered him. It was bad faith and she deserved better. He would not bring up the subject himself, but omissions can be falsehoods, too. To make things even worse, he understood that girls back then (and even now) were often thinking practical thoughts about marriage and children. Not immediately, necessarily, but in the not too distant future. It was a factor in their calculations. That he was now occupied in exactly this same kind of thinking was uncomfortable, but it might well have prompted him to see their relationship from her point of view. If he loved her, did he not owe her this basic decency? At least he wanted not to be a shit.

(As a matter of fact, although he couldn't have known it at the time, she did meet a graduate student in her junior year and married him a week after her graduation. Of course she got married. A beautiful, sexy girl like that? When he learned of it, he remembered his high-mindedness and regretted its accuracy.)

It was depressing and insoluble, and he was unutterably lonely. The abrupt descent from delight to torment left him giddy. Simple tasks that had been automatic now required attention and willpower. He had to order himself to do trivial things like brushing his teeth. This was, as far as he can remember, his first experience of suffering. There would be others, but as their various strands wound themselves together, this particular filament would always be there to remind him not just of her or of them but of the world's imperfections. Whatever other griefs he might experience, this would always be a part of their composition.

An exaggeration? Are you not sentimentalizing?

No, he insists. He would not continue forever in deep mourning for her, but his losing her would always remind him both of her and of his defects of character for once he had recognized the category, he had no doubt that other unattractive examples would manifest themselves. This was only the harbinger of many more.

It was also undeniable that the longer he waited, the worse it would be, the more painful, surely, but also worse, morally. Worse for her. He wanted to be an ornament to what he hoped would be her elegant life, not a lasting cause of regret. That might sound suspiciously noble, but he was in love with her, remember. And he could only suppose that she felt something like that for him. The separation would be wrenching. 'Love me or leave me / and let me forget you.' That was from a song in the movie of that name about Ruth Etting. It is the only movie he can remember their seeing together. With Doris Day, for God's sake, and James Cagney.

Their song, then? That would be too much. But life is often too much. Whenever he heard it, he thought of her.

THERE WAS, LOGICALLY, ANOTHER POSSIBLE SOLUTION. He could end the relationship with Leah—because her behavior and her attitude did not bode well for the long term or, less tactfully, because she had been such a pain in the ass. They weren't engaged or even engaged to be engaged. But if she was now demanding an exclusive relationship, that was clearly on the table. In the cards. (Aren't the cards always on the table?) He could not imagine a worse way for her to have proposed such a change in their relationship. So, he could break off with her while, unrelatedly, ending the affair with Jenny—for her good, knowing how dim their prospects were. He thought about it and could see that this might be the correct thing to do, appropriate for each and all. It was a painful realization. Losing either one of them would be regrettable; breaking it off with both would be a catastrophe. All his assurance and happiness would disappear and on a more basic level he would be diminished to...celibacy. Which is worse than virginity, because celibates, some of them anyway, know what they're missing. But he would miss their company, too, their conversation, and their laughter. In different tones and timbres, of course, but both delightful. They were his best friends and he could not imagine that there could be others who could take their places. (There haven't been many.)

Stupid? Yes. The entire approach was wrong, reasoning and quantifying about a thing that was unreasonable and incommensurate. That was the kind of thinking he had been educated to do but here it was useless and misguided. Nowhere is it written (by anyone smart, that is) that the mind is equal to the challenges experience sets before it. All I can say on his behalf is that he knows better now, when it is decades too late and altogether irrelevant. To listen to the faint promptings of the spirit is only possible when a person realizes that he has a spirit and that, at least in some things, it is the only trustworthy authority.

There was a glimmer of hope. Why couldn't he keep going with Jenny and then, when they came to the cantilever part of the bridge, if indeed they got that far and the bridge was there, cross it. Maybe by then he would have developed more courage. Surely he would be less dependent on his parents for money. He might not go to graduate school, even if that could leave him vulnerable to the draft. But that would be happening to many of his classmates. Would he have the bravery (bravado) for such a departure from the plans his parents had made for him? They may not have been his own plans but they were conventional and safe and had been in his head for years. To tell himself that he was going to end it with Jenny for *her* sake would be even less convincing to her than it was to him. She would snort (he could almost hear it) but with contempt rather than amusement.

At last, the churning subsided and he recognized that whatever he did and whichever way he chose, it would turn out to be the wrong thing. About that realization, he felt a surprising certainty. It was a depressing discovery but in some ways a relief as well, because it took some of the onus from him. If any decision was going to be wrong, then it didn't matter so much what he did. Admit powerlessness and mindlessness, and the worst choice might very well be the best. Choice itself might be an illusion. It was unknowable. Out of his hands. His mistake had been in thinking that he had any say in how his life was going to progress. That was what his classmates thought, most of them children of privilege who had been protected all their lives. And it might even apply to some of the athletes, the big men on campus, the heirs of great wealth who could assume that they, too, would enjoy these blessings. And they would, if they didn't fuck up too badly. But for him? No. Get rid of both, then. Start fresh. That was what he would do because, frighteningly, satisfyingly, it was the most terrible option.

WITH LEAH, IT WAS EASY. He didn't have to do or even say anything. The next move was his and if it took him a while to decide (which was what she would think at first) that was fine. Then as his silence extended itself, her confidence would begin to crumble. He could not believe that she didn't care. (Why else would she have been possessive enough to demand that he get rid of Jenny?) So it stood to reason that she would be waiting for a phone call or a letter, some signal that he had decided to comply with her wishes. Impatiently at first and then, gradually with less and less confidence. Weeks? Months? The longer it took, the better, because the more she loved him, the stupider was her insistence that he choose and the more peremptory was her changing of the rules. He could even imagine that she might eventually call or write to withdraw her ridiculous demands. It wasn't likely but not impossible.

He lay in bed in the darkness of his dorm room, unable to fall asleep and diverting himself with variations on what could now happen. He might forget about Leah but not entirely, not permanently, and show up in a year or two—if only to infuriate her. No, that might not be so good. He didn't want to give her the chance to reject him, even under those weird circumstances.

These weren't real scenarios he was composing for himself. Call them daydreams, except that this was at night. Laurel and Hardy are carrying a grand piano across a rope bridge, okay? And from the other direction, a gorilla starts to cross. What do they do? That kind of thing is only a diversion. (Do gorillas ever use rope bridges? And to whom in the deep jungle are the comedians delivering a piano?)

The more he considered what to do, the more annoyed he got with Leah, and the fonder he felt of Jenny. Did he really have to break up with her? Could he? Was he doing this for her good or his own? Wouldn't it be better to treat her as a grown-up, a responsible person who could look after herself? They'd never discussed marriage. How could he tell whether she was using him as someone who was safe, which is to say outside the marriage pool? (No, he couldn't believe that. It had no relation to the Jenny he knew.)

He'd go up there to Cambridge and they'd talk about it. He would tell her about his feeling of duplicitousness that he could not get rid of. He'd explain to her the lengths to which his parents would go to 'save' him. They hadn't said a word yet, but he knew they would. He was as certain of that as he was of his inability to withstand their onslaught. Fundamentally, he was left feeling unworthy of Jenny.

Why couldn't he have been grateful for that? Why feel guilty about something that hadn't happened? (Guilt without wrongdoing is very Jewy but he couldn't help himself.) He shakes his head and says that he should have known better. He should at least have been honest with himself about what he wanted and willing to fight for it, at whatever risk. So he was lacking not only in character but intellect. These are awkward categories for a kid to deal with. In a brief while the guilt gave way to a numb hopelessness. Petrarch? Shakespeare? Donne? They all have a lot to say about these situations and he'd read their poems, but they were like seeds on the surface that had not yet had time to take root or touch his life. He was in a *selva oscura* and could not see his way. He decided that he might as well put himself in her hands and let her decide. The worst that could happen was that she would agree with him. There would be nothing more to lose.

And? And? Surely he must have remembered this. But no, it, too, is a blur. He has the idea that they might have had dinner together at the Hong Kong on Mass. Avenue—'the Kong,' as the kids call it now—but that could have been another time that he's conflating. His brain just isn't very good anymore. (Was it ever?) You remember that wonderful moment in Proust where a loose cobblestone in a courtyard brings Marcel back to an earlier occasion? Our dufus could trip, fall down, bloody his nose—on the very same stone in the very same place—and have no recollection whatsoever that it had happened sixty years before.

But, okay, it was probably dinner, and certainly up there in Cambridge, either at the Hong Kong or somewhere else. (The Dolphin? Was that in business back then? The square is now all banks and optical shops, so that its memory of itself has faded, too.) What he said, he is fairly certain, was something like what we have been talking about. He can make out the E at the top of the chart, or thinks he can, because he knows without looking. Jewish, yaya-ya, parents, lalala, holocaust, wawawa, unfair (not that the holocaust was unfair but it would be unfair of him to take up her time and diminish her opportunities for better matches elsewhere), shit, bastard, dope (those were names he called himself) and the too predictable rest of it. To which he can remember her response, which was laughter, and, 'You're out of your mind!'

Not quite what he had expected but accurate in its way.

'I wish I were,' he said, or some such thing. 'I'm serious.'

'I don't believe you. Not for a fucking minute.'

Eventually, their talk subsided into a baleful silence. Bale? It's an old German word meaning 'terrible' or 'evil.' Whether or not she believed this intermarriage foolishness, it was clear enough to her that the general import of the conversation was that he was dumping her and that they wouldn't be seeing each other anymore. They had been having a wonderful time together and now it was just going to stop? Apparently. She finished the lukewarm tea in her little cup, set it down on the table, and left him sitting there. No, she didn't want him to walk her back to the dorm. What in hell for?

UP UNTIL THIS MOMENT, it had all been speculative. Thinking, as we come to realize, doesn't mean much. This was an act, however, and action does carry meaning, although we may not realize it at the moment. It is difficult for me to like this fellow, and therefore something of a stretch to feel sympathy for him. He screwed up his life? Well, people do that. But most of them shrug and forget about it. Here, he is different. It is his regret over the course of decades that perhaps earns him a modicum of pity. He was stupid, but sorrow, if it endures long enough, has its shabby dignity. If I thought he was altogether detestable, I'd have quit long before this and left him to his own devices. Think of him as a physician thinks of a patient: he may not be an interesting fellow but his malady can be fascinating and even instructive.

HE PUZZLED IT OUT on the way back to New Haven. She was too decent a person, too free of bigotry herself, to suspect it in others. She must have assumed that he was telling her an absurd story in order to break up with her for some altogether different and more banal reason. Why hadn't he thought of that before? But what good would it have done him if he had?

Before, he had felt numb. Now he realized that before was only the Novocaine and this was the gas. This was beyond numb and into insensibility. It had been terrible. She had been fine and he had been terrible. He blamed himself but Leah, too, for having put him in this predicament. In the following days and weeks, he drank rather more than usual although he never got really blotto. (Nice Jewish boys don't do that!) He applied himself to his course work, amused by the fact that this was exactly what his father would want him to do. As if that mattered. As if anything mattered.

The only difference in his life was that he had to buy an alarm clock. He had been an early riser, up at first light. Now, bed was a good place to hide and he would roll over and snooze sometimes, missing his morning classes. He got himself a cheap clock, a Big Ben with a loud ring and a thunderous ticking he had to listen to at night, hammering away with its perseverant accusation. If he'd been in a double or a quad, he could have asked one of his roommates to rouse him. But he was in a single, in solitary, just him and that water-torture clock.

HE RESENTED LEAH but he also resented his parents, who had never said a word and hadn't known what part they had played in the negotiations that had been going on in his head. He was doing what they wanted, not gadding off on weekends to women's colleges but dutifully studying in his room, catching up on reading, preparing papers ahead of time so that he could proofread them, and drinking a lot of coffee. Black, of course. His surrender was all the more shameful because it had come before the attack. He supposed that this anger toward them was irrational. He also thought it was temporary and would fade sooner or later, dissolving into the ordinary bitterness of family life. That he agreed with them at least in part only made his indignation worse. Silence, exile, and cunning are what Joyce recommends. If exile was out of the question and cunning was beyond him, he could at least rely on silence. He crossed Gothic or handsome Georgian quadrangles that were full of students and felt as though he were the only person among all those robots, or, perhaps, he was the robot and they were the people. The only relief he could imagine was to stop thinking entirely, which is hard to do. Zen masters spend a lifetime in the effort and, while he wasn't seriously planning to attempt it, he could understand for the first time what it was that they were trying to do. Unhappiness comes from desire? So stop desiring! You can starve to death that way or perish of thirst but in theory you don't care. Very probably you will lose weight. (Have you ever seen a fat Zen master?) But you won't care about that either.

His expectation that the pain would diminish or that he would somehow become inured to it turned out to be correct, although the diminution was very slow. He kept thinking about both girls, Jenny more than Leah, not just because he had lost her but because he had behaved badly to her. He tried to imagine an alternate universe in which that last encounter had come out differently, or had never happened, or in which one could undo it as with a Magic Slate. But he knew that any alternate universe is one of dreams and desires and no one can go there.

THE SHARP, STABBING PAINS dulled to a steady ache and he was beginning to think he'd get through it after all, when Leah called one Thursday evening not to ask him but tell him that they should have dinner together in New York on Saturday. They had a lot to talk about.

'Do we?'

'Don't we?' she asked. 'But that's not a reason for you to come. I can see that. The only reason for you to be there would be because you want to. Do you?'

A quick frisson of satisfaction: she had waited until she couldn't wait anymore. This was, if he wanted to look at it that way, her surrender if not quite his victory.

'I don't know.'

'Then there's nothing left to say, is there?' she asked.

He realized that she was about to hang up. Did he want that?

'Wait,' he said.

Did he want that? He was surprised at having blurted it out without any forethought. (So much for reason. So much for planning. So much for will.)

They went to dinner at one of those inexpensive French restaurants there used to be in the west fifties and then back to her aunt's townhouse where they could make love savagely on the couch in the basement den, which is not exactly surprising. (They say a prick has no conscience, but it also seems to be lacking in intelligence.) When she came, she cried out loudly enough so that he worried that her aunt upstairs might hear them. Also, with her orgasm, she farted, which she'd never done before and which he took as a kind of compliment. Leah was good looking and had a dark bosomy beauty, a little like Suzanne Pleshette's. She had a mercurial range of emotions but even at her worst contrived to turn her sullenness to advantage, so that it made her unpredictable and intriguing. Or so he thought. A more sensible person might have read the warning signs, of which even he was dimly aware, but there was the other and far more vivid side of it, the mystery, if that's not too high-flown a word. And the sex. He never knew quite where he was with her but that was fascinating. He'd never known anyone like this before. (But how many women had he known before? What experience had he had? He was a kid, remember, and this was exciting. He was, after all, a sucker for education.) It is also worth pointing out that while twenty-year-old girls are women, twenty-year-old boys are still boys. Then and now. And the women know it, and the boys don't. (Mostly, they don't know anything.)

They resumed 'seeing' each other, which he didn't think was necessarily a commitment to anything. Not to her, surely. But in a strange way to Judaism, or at least it was an assertion of some Jewish identity he'd never before realized he had in him. This bizarre idea allowed him to share the responsibility for his decision with his parents, so that he could live with them and himself. This revelation (Jews have revelations, don't they?) was slow to manifest itself and, had it been announced from some burning bush, he might have laughed at it and dismissed it as *mishegas*. But it was an alternative to anger at Leah and, for aesthetic reasons, he preferred not to feel that. As long as he was fucking her, he wanted to be on at least amicable terms. He didn't have the toughness or honesty to admit that he was just fucking her. 'Taking advantage of her' is the old-fashioned phrase, but that implies that it's a bad thing. It does happen, however. He had been too finicky to do that with Jenny. And paradoxically, loving Leah less, he felt his obligation more keenly.

(Remember that kid crossing the courtyard some pages ago to whom I wanted to call out warnings? Here, I want to grab him by the shoulders, shake him, and yell at him that's he's a moron, a cesspool of received ideas that are mostly false, the victim of a phony high-mindedness that isn't even in his character. He doesn't notice and just keeps on walking, putting one foot in front of the other in those fashionably scuffed, white buckskin shoes.)

The resumption of the affair with Leah—his choice of her over Jenny—was like a Bar Mitzvah, but different in tone from most of them. More realistic, surely. We think of Bar Mitzvahs as happy occasions and everybody pretends it is a great treat to be a Jew, something to celebrate with feasting and dancing and presents. It can be happy but there ought to be a note of sadness in it, too, a recognition of the weight of apartness that is being placed on the frail shoulders of a thirteen-year-old. This reconnection with his 'heritage' felt closer to the truth, a recognition of status he had earned that was not without great costs. This was harder to learn than any *haftorah*. His decision not to try to battle his parents, to yield to what he knew would be overwhelming force, and to terminate his affair with Jenny had been heartbreaking but it was also a recognition of who he was. And couldn't help being? At the time, he thought not. (He might have been less dissatisfied if this Judaism business had brought him any peace, or acceptance, or willingness to submit to the whims of God, but it didn't. He wasn't ready for that then—and isn't now.)

One who leaves Judaism is called an *apikoros*. Which means an apostate and a heretic. It is the Hebrew form of Epicurus, the brilliant philosopher whose views Lucretius expresses so well in *The Nature of Things*. He wouldn't have wanted to admit it, but he was a lot closer to Lucretius than to the Five Books of Moses, more a follower of Spinoza than of Maimonides. He had not been brought up to wind phylacteries, obey commandments, pray three times a day, and avoid not only pork and shellfish but the wearing of linen and wool at the same time. Who, beside himself, was he trying to fool?

They got married soon after graduation. To live happily ever after? Come on, get serious. That doesn't even happen in novels anymore. In fairy tales, maybe, but the children, too smart to believe in them, realize that it's a mere convention. Or maybe it happens in one of those alternate universes, the doorway to which sometimes seems to be open a tantalizing crack.

2

AND THE MARRIAGE? How was that?

He hesitated and then answered, thoughtfully I thought. (Why lie to your own narrator, after all? There may be unreliable narrators, but characters should say what they mean, or what they think they mean.) 'It was a marriage. Ups and downs. It lasted a long time, comparatively. Twenty years, almost. And it ended with bad feeling on both sides, as one expects. Otherwise, divorces would make no sense. But this isn't about Leah. It's about me. And Jenny. And the decision I made.'

Leah isn't even relevant?

'Of course she's relevant. But I was the one who decided, or thought I had. If the marriage had turned out to be twenty years of Norman Rockwell bliss, that might have alleviated some of the shame I felt about how badly I had behaved to Jenny. Or, as I came to see it, toward us, Jenny and myself. Uninterrupted family tranquility would at least have been an anodyne. It could have seemed like an endorsement of my choice, in practical terms anyway, and would have made my decision look better. But life is not that generous. Leah continued to assert her independence in increasingly distressing ways. (The distress wasn't accidental. She had the feminist movement on her side with its social and political description of guys like me, or maybe all guys everywhere, as oppressors. I shouldn't have been surprised. When it got bad, I would think of Jenny and what a fool I'd been. Wounds, self-inflicted ones especially, continue to hurt for a long time.'

Did you keep in touch with Jenny, then?

'No. I was ashamed to. And didn't have the nerve. Besides, I'd heard that she'd married and gone off to Africa somewhere. Africa doesn't have a phone book.'

You thought of her?

'Oh, yes. Not obsessively but not infrequently either.'

IT IS AN INTERESTING TECHNICAL PROBLEM to try to make a character like him attractive. How to begin? He is not such a worthless and pusillanimous fellow as he thinks—or says he thinks. He was for most of those years a good enough husband and an okay father. He worked in city planning and then, as the endless wrangles with politicians and businessmen that are part of the profession took some of the shine off his youthful idealism, he went over to the dark side. He knew from his training and practical experience which way a city was likely to develop, which areas were likely to decay and which might revive and flourish. And he saw what was obvious— that there was money to be made if he could anticipate the behavior of the market by a year or two. It was chancy but less so than the stock market. And his knowledge made his prospects better than those of a naïve player who lets his hopes cloud his judgment. What he was able to do was combine certain facts, some of them obvious and others subtle, that could be relevant to the choices people made. In most cities, London and Paris for instance, the west side with the afternoon light is the fashionable part. But in Manhattan, with the blustery wind that comes roaring down the Hudson in the winter to pummel Riverside Drive and West End Avenue and all those cross streets, the West Side never blossomed the way it was supposed to and it remained, for many years, slightly cheaper, more intellectual, more ethnic. Pieces of information like that were useful but not sufficient—one also needs accurate hunches, and he had these, too. He and a few partners made some investments together and did well, and then very well.

Business took him away from home for weeks at a time and that, paradoxically, may have helped prolong the marriage. It is unnecessary to argue with someone a thousand miles away. He missed a few school plays, maybe, but he could tell himself he was doing it for them and hope that they would understand—although children never do.

He co-wrote a book about forecasting the decay and occasional regeneration of areas of cities and the consequent fluctuation of property values in urban real estate. It was the idea of one of his partners that they do a book together, because sitting alone in their hotel rooms was tedious. They could collaborate on this to occupy the time. So, mostly as a favor to the friend—Henry Mittenthal—he participated, sending off a chapter for Henry to review, and then reviewing the next chapter that Henry sent him. It was interesting to clarify their thoughts that way and not excessively laborious. When it was done, they sent it to a publisher who promptly accepted it, paid them a more than respectable advance, and brought it out the following spring, a good-looking volume with which he was pleased. The money was nice, the book was handsome, and the project was fun, which he realized he hadn't had in a while.

It kept on being fun in unexpected ways. His and Henry's reputations as real-estate gurus were enhanced and that was good for business. What he hadn't anticipated was that they would be interviewed by print journalist and invited to appear on talk-radio and TV. His publisher flew him to New York and put him up at the St Regis so he and Henry could appear on an 'important' morning talk show. Silly, but amusing. George Brett, the great third baseman for the Royals, happened to be on the same program in another segment and, during a commercial break he asked to borrow someone's ballpoint pen so he could autograph a baseball for the host. Our lucky protagonist had one and produced it. That was something he could tell his kids.

There was also an author of some book about mindfulness scheduled for the following segment, and she had her publicist with her. (He wondered why their publisher hadn't provided such a person for him and Henry.) He saw them for only an instant as the production assistant led him from the green room onto the set. He turned back to look again. Yes. The publicist was Jenny. Should he say something? Wait for her to say something? But there was no time. The production person led him and Henry onto the set to be fitted with lapel-mikes. They were on for six minutes. He had no idea what he'd said, or even if he'd said anything. Mostly he let Henry talk, nodding thoughtfully, agreeing, and trying not to seem stupid. His attention was elsewhere.

At the end of their segment he had to choose once more. Just leave the studio or go back to the green room where he knew she would be waiting for her author to be called? It would be cowardly not to go. And rude. She'd know. Even if she hadn't noticed him as they'd passed each other, she would know that he'd been on the program and, if he cut her this way, would have yet another reason to feel contempt for him. (Assuming that he still mattered at all to her. Assuming that she even remembered him.) (But how could she not?) He told Henry he'd catch him later and marched back there.

He had no idea what to expect except that this reunion would be very brief and probably painful. That was what he deserved, wasn't it? If the Fates had contrived this encounter, it had to be to hurt him. Do unto others and sooner or later they will do it unto you. But then even the most humiliating few minutes would be better than nothing. The best he could hope for was that he had never been all that important to her. (No!) Or that enough time had passed so that the young man and young woman they had been were now no more than tiny figures off in the distance close to the vanishing point. What did he want? He had no clear idea. His heart was beating rapidly—not the romantic locus of emotion but the banausic organ that pumps blood. It is more modest but more reliable.

The door was open. He looked in. 'Jenny,' he said. Not interrogatively. Nor in surprise. It was as flat as he could make it, because he had no idea what response to expect.

She had little time to react. A different production assistant had come to fetch her and her author. Jenny glanced at him for an instant and said, 'Wait,' meaning, he supposed, that he should wait for her to return after their piece of the show.

'I will,' he said. And then, having no idea where the words came from, 'I have been.'

SHE HAD AGED. People do over the course of thirty years. But she still looked good. Crisp, in the manner of professional women. Beautifully turned out with a very good suit, Louis Ferraud maybe, and hair and maquillage one could only describe as authoritative. A little heavier in the hips, perhaps, but that happens to women. Still, she carried herself regally. He was happy to see her looking so good and had the exhilarating sense that he knew the body. He wished he had paid more attention to his own, had put in some time in a gym, or at least had paid more attention to his clothing. He was afraid that she would be disappointed. Afraid? Yes, it was like being young again, nervous, self-conscious, and tongue-tied. The strange thing was that it felt good, just as it had felt good to be twenty.

He left the empty green room to go back to the studio floor where, standing well behind the cameras, he could see her and even gaze as she watched her author, judging, evaluating, and preparing to make suggestions for her next appearance. She was focused entirely on the show, so he could stare without her knowing it. As he studied her, he saw that she wasn't merely a woman, or even an attractive woman with whom he had been in love once, but a figure from another world, from that altogether different life he could have chosen. And would have lived. Not perfect, of course. No lives are. But the highs and lows would have had a different texture and a different idiolect. Over the years husbands and wives develop their own shared language, full of private references and allusions, as if they were speaking in poetry rather than the mere prose they use with the rest of the world. He had no idea what the discourse would have been like over the years between Jenny and him but it was sobering to realize that this would have been his mother tongue. He could not retrieve particular remarks she had made all those years ago but he remembered the flavor of her banter, her wisecracks, her mood shifts. It would have been a beautifully complicated and richly inflected language.

When the interview was finished and the producer of the show was escorting Jenny and her writer toward the exit, they passed by where he was standing. She hardly paused but told him the name of a bar and a designated a time—six o'clock. What bar? He doesn't remember. He has walked back and forth on those streets many times in the years that have elapsed, but it isn't there anymore. All he can bring back is that it was a quiet place in art deco with deep black leather chairs at glass and chrome tables. He nodded yes, but she hadn't waited for his answer. She had just assumed, which was encouraging. No, it was the fact that she had appointed a place and time to meet that was encouraging. Was splendid! He watched her walk with her author toward the elevators and considered hurrying to catch up with them. But that wasn't what she had invited him to do. She wanted privacy, perhaps? That could be good, too.

HE WENT BACK TO HIS HOTEL to lie down and think. First of all, he had to change his flight back to Albuquerque, putting it off a day. Then he had to decide whether to extend his hotel stay by a day. He should do that even if, against all odds and beyond reason, she invited him to spend the night with her. He certainly couldn't count on that, could hardly even imagine it, but he had a moment of magical thinking in which he decided that if he paid for an extra night he wouldn't need the room but if he just checked out and left his luggage with the bellman, he would. Stupid, but what isn't? When in Cloudcuckooland, you cannot ignore the cuckoos.

Even to be considering that remote possibility of being welcomed back into her life was an occasion for rejoicing. If she could forgive him, there might be a way for him eventually to forgive himself. And what was most reassuring was her undemonstrative but decisive reaction to his presence there. 'Wait.' And then the name of a bar and a time. Not even, 'Hello.' Curious. Is this how love scenes go? Her words had been few but clear. Had she smiled? He couldn't remember. Less that an hour ago and it was already fading away. The Japanese tourists are right to go around taking pictures and videos of everything. They're not missing the trip because there isn't any. The video is the trip, because, as they understand, mere experience trickles away almost at once from even the most attentive mind, leaving at best a faint redolence of what seemed at the time to be real.

What if she invited him for more than a night? Would he want that? Was he ready for it? He and Leah were divorced and he lived with Caroline now, had been with her almost three years. Was he prepared to abandon her and Albuquerque, pick up, and move to New York? Was he any braver now than he had been as a youngster?

Neither Jenny nor Caroline were Jewish, but his parents were dead and that old business didn't matter anymore. Start over then? The question wouldn't come up. It wasn't possible. But if? He took a shower, in case. And while the water was streaming down on him, he looked down at his body and saw how much he had deteriorated from his twenty-year-old self, his gut now sagging a little, not quite in a paunch but indicating what he could expect in not so many years. He also rehearsed things he might say to her. The protestations of love would be easy; the confessions about how wrong he had been would be harder.

He was afraid either way. Not of Jenny or even of himself, but of life and its choices, ultimately more imperious than any Leah ever have imagined. He lay down on the bed to rest and fell asleep.

HE GOT TO THE BAR a little before six. Eager, yes, but also considerate: he didn't want her to have to wait for him. He expected that she might be a bit late. She was coming from work, after all. And women are often a little late anyway. That was what he'd do in her place. It was good of her to see him, but she wouldn't want to let him to think it was especially important to her.

Evidence for this?

'None. But it's what I was thinking. I couldn't help it. She was, after all this time—thirty years almost—largely a figment and therefore unknowable. I was imagining various possibilities that might help me get a better read on what she said and didn't say.'

Call it reasonable unreason. It is hard to blame him. He was under some stress. His mind was racing. His hands were cold. A waiter asked him what he wanted and he said he was waiting for someone. Then on second thought he decided to order if only to have a glass to hold in his hand. A gin-and-bitters, maybe.

You remember that? What you drank?

'Not really. All I remember is that it was ordinary. When she arrived the waiter asked if she wanted her usual. She nodded. The usual turned out to be St James Rhum on ice with a wedge of lime. She might have developed a taste for it when she was living in Paris, which she did for a few years. It's from Martinique, but I think they grow the sugar cane there and export it to France where they actually make the rum. Or rhum. I remember that.'

Remember that they make the rhum in France?

'No. I remember what she was drinking.'

Were you drinking pink gin back then?

'I don't remember. Maybe, not. But it was ordinary. If it wasn't gin, it was probably scotch. Johnny Walker Black, I'd imagine. My drink isn't important. It was hers that impressed me. I don't think I've ever seen anyone else order that.'

And you mention this, why?

'Back when we were in college, when she was a sophomore and I was a senior, I was the older one, the one who knew things. Not about grand subjects, of course, but what to drink. Now our positions had changed. I was the kid and she was the sophisticated, experienced woman. She was the glamorous one and I had had the lower case life. I remember that flashed in my mind.'

The waiter brought her the rum and lime and he raised his glass of whatever it was. She raised hers and they clinked glasses in a kind of toast.

'What's to say?' she asked.

'No idea,' he said. 'Everything. Nothing. 'Here's looking at you kid'? Will that do?'

She shook her head no, but took a sip. He noticed her beautiful fingernails. Artifice, but very impressive. My God, she had turned out well.

They talked. He can't remember the words or even the order in which the subjects came up. She told him that she had married and then divorced someone named Douglas. She'd had two daughters. They had lived in Nairobi, Addis Ababa, Paris, and Geneva at various times. After the divorce, she and the daughters—she must have named them for him but he has forgotten—returned to New York. Then she gave an eloquent shrug, as if to say that none of this was special or interesting. (Compared to what, he asked himself. It sounded rich and exotic. And look at her!) He told her about himself, marriage, children, and divorce. Flying around the country like some raptor scanning below for food, except that his prey was cities in which he could make money for himself and his partners. What it meant was that he was essentially rootless. Or he was like those banyan trees that drop roots from their branches and connect wherever they can to whatever is below.

'That's fanciful,' she said. And then, 'You haven't changed much.'

Oh, yes. He'd changed. He'd aged and been beaten down some from that cocky kid she had known. He had learned for one thing what a blunder it had been to let her go. And there was no way to go back. Terrible.

'Yes,' she agreed. It wasn't entirely clear whether she was agreeing that it was terrible for him or was, perhaps, including herself. Or she could just have meant that there was no going back. Any of these interpretations was grammatically possible.

She finished her drink. 'Another?' he offered.

'Come on home,' she said. 'I have booze there. We'll order take-out Chinese.'

'Fine,' he said, not altogether certain that he'd heard right or that it wasn't some kind of joke.

His signaled to the waiter for a check, but she told him she had an account here and that the company paid for it.

IT SOUNDS CONTRIVED, I know. Or perhaps the better word would be unbelievable. It was as though he were watching an opera having previously read the libretto, but now with the music and sets. Or anyway, the sense perceptions—the taste of the gin (let's say it was gin) and the faint scent of her perfume. (L'Heure bleu?)

He tried to pay for the taxi to her apartment on West End Avenue, but she insisted. She said she had a cab allowance from the company for evenings. And a car came for her in the mornings. He didn't argue but followed her into the lobby and up to her apartment. She opened the door. It was a big old-fashioned place with high ceilings and fine wide-board floors. He noticed a man's hat, a snappy looking porkpie with a red feather in the band, on a bentwood coat rack in the hall. 'Yours?'

'No. His.' She lived with a black tenor sax player who was on the road a lot. Prominent if not quite famous outside of the jazz world. He'd never heard of him.

'Drink?'

'Sure.'

She kept her St James' in the freezer. He had one, too. She cut up a lime, put a wedge in each glass, and handed him one. 'To us,' she said.

They drank. It was oaky.

'She took a step toward him. 'Kiss me, you fool!'

Surely you're making that up.

'No, I swear. How could I forget it? And it was so unexpected. I could never decide whether she meant I was a fool for not kissing her or more generally.'

He kissed her. They kissed. They took their drinks into the bedroom and continued, shedding their clothing slowly to draw out the anticipation. They settled down onto the bed and were eager, even hungry, as they reunited. Also sad. At least he was, because this astonishing sweetness was what he had been missing all those years. What a dolt!

They lay together afterward, holding each other, not needing to say anything, at least for that moment. After a while, though, he was unable to keep the words back, corny and banal as he knew they sounded, even if true: 'I love you. Always have. All along.'

'I know.' And then, her rueful smile brightened. 'I'm hungry. I'll call for dinner.'

She got out of bed and walked to the bathroom for her robe. He admired the curves of her back. Why a robe? He figured that, sooner or later, she'd have to answer the door for the delivery. Still it was a shame for such gorgeousness to cover itself.

It was a white figured silk robe that made her look, again, like the formidable woman of the TV studio and the bar. Elegant. Like the Marschallin in *Rosenkavalier*. She sat on the edge of the bed, looked down at him, and asked, 'So what happened to us?'

'I was a coward. I couldn't face the struggle with my parents. It makes no sense now, but they're dead and I'm old enough not to worry anymore about what they thought.'

'That's what you said then. I didn't believe it. Anti-Semitism is one thing, but anti-gentilism? Is there such a thing?'

'Not so much now, I think. But there was.'

She shook her head, either as a negative or just in wonder. 'But they didn't mind that you were seeing me, did they?'

'They didn't take you seriously. They couldn't imagine a future for us and thought—this sounds terrible but it's true—that your being a gentile somehow made it safe.'

'They would only have been upset, then, if we'd got married? Or engaged?'

'Something like that.'

'But we never talked about marriage! We could have gone on the way we were. For years. Forever!'

'I didn't think of it.'

' You could have asked me. Did that ever cross your little mind? We could have talked it over. How could you make a decision like that on your own?'

'I don't know. Stupid.'

She shook her head. 'Hopelessly middle class, is what it was,' she said. 'And we both thought you were so smart.'

She picked up the drink she'd left on the nightstand. They must have talked more, but he can't remember much of it. After her divorce, she'd had to get a job and, through a friend of her mother's, found a publishing house that needed someone to work in publicity. She was good at it and rose through the ranks like some Horatio Alger heroine (if he'd had heroines). What sticks in his mind with clarity is that when the bell rang to announce the delivery from the Chinese restaurant, he reached for his pants to extract money, but she smiled and shook her head, no. 'You got the last one,' she said.

'The last one?'

'At the Hong Kong. You remember.'

Jesus! 'Yes,' he said. 'It never goes away. It was inexcusable.'

'It was.'

He had to keep himself from groaning. He even managed to maintain something like the same expression on his face.

She went to the hall to receive the delivery.

'This is too messy for bed,' she called back. 'Come into the kitchen.'

He put on his undershorts—she was still in her robe—and went out to join her.

THE FOOD. . . . He has forgotten. He couldn't recall what they'd had at the Hong Kong either and wonders whether she had remembered and these were the same choices. Probably not, but, alas, it wasn't impossible. They ate, he with a fork and she with chopsticks. Then she poured some good brandy into snifters and they went back to bed. Make love again? He was worried a little because he wasn't a kid anymore. But she wasn't insistent. They lay together with their brandies on their chests. He noticed her long narrow feet and their perfect toenails with clear lacquer on them. Noticed and remembered. Feet don't change much. After a while, she turned the light off and they lay together in the dark, still talking but with longer pauses between the sentences. That was when she surprised him a little, saying that he used to have names for her breasts. 'Remember?'

'No. Sorry.' (Kid stuff, but they were kids then and kids do sappy things. What names would have been reasonable? Tosca and Aida? Veronica and Betty? Maria Theresa and Marie Antoinette?) He salvaged his memory lapse—mammary lapse? —as well as he could by kissing them. He remembered one of his English masters at prep school making fun of Walter Benton's terrible poem in *This is My Beloved*, quoting the ridiculous line, 'I kissed her breasts, one by one,' which, as the teacher pointed out, would be the most convenient way to do it.

For a woman who had had two children, the breasts were in fine shape, the aureoles maybe a shade darker than he remembered, not strawberry sorbet anymore but a light mocha. But to notice that wasn't to disapprove. Lovely!

At some point, she yawned, which could have been a comment or just a yawn. She got up and made her way to the bathroom without turning the light on in order not to wake him if he was asleep. She left the door open, as she might have if they were an old married couple. When she flushed and returned to bed, he got up and groped his way through the unfamiliar room to the toilet. He got back into bed, snuggled next to her, and thought about that married couple they might have been and the lives they might have had together. Take their affair in college and make that one point, and then take this moment as a second point, and one could, at least in theory, plot a line....

She lay with her head on his shoulder and almost instantly fell asleep, or so it seemed from her breathing. He could feel her delicate exhalations as they reached his skin. He knew that sooner or later, with her head on his arm, he would be uncomfortable, but that, too, was a privilege. What more can one ask for in this life?

He may have dozed off for a while but he soon woke to feel the nerves of his left arm beginning to go numb. He had to move. As gently as he could, he shifted his body, and she adjusted herself but as she did so put her hand and arm across his abdomen where it stayed for a few minutes before moving down to his genitals, which she just held, the way a little girl might hold a Teddy bear for security. A learned behavior, he imagined, but what difference did that make? He had been impressed long ago by Edmund Wilson's description of this in *Memoirs of Hecate County*. She could have picked it up from there, although that was hardly likely. At any rate if felt fine. He lay there enjoying it.

She was asleep, he supposed, and that was nice. He fell asleep, too. An hour or so later—he had no idea how much time had passed—he awoke. Her hand was still on his penis, which he was surprised and pleased to discover was erect. He reached over to Marie Antoinette and kissed her. And they made quiet, almost tantric love, barely moving, so that he could imagine the cessation of time itself, which was what he profoundly wanted. To stay there with her, just like this, without moving, without saying anything, forever. It was, he knew, an impossibility, but he could imagine it. They couldn't go back all those years, but next best would be to stay here this way with her in an infinitely protracted present. Orgasm? What man wouldn't want one eventually? But he also dreaded it because he knew it would mean that all the clocks in the world would start ticking again.

Some men will claim to be creatures of the Enlightenment and to have no pangs of conscience about such adventures as this. They are telling the truth but not all of it, because there is a moment, usually at four in the morning, when there is a judgment the mind makes (or the body's mind), expressing its reservations and asking the painful question: *What in hell am I doing here?* But it can sometimes inflict an even greater pain by showing approval and announcing unequivocally that *This feels like home,* so that even in the bed, with his naked body next to hers, he regrets the separation and the loss that are so clearly impending. He may reach out to put his palm on the smooth warmth of her hip, but he knows that this is temporary and that they will lose touch. Must they? Must he? Isn't there some way to rearrange his life, their lives?

The brief interval of wakefulness passed and he fell back to sleep, but then the sun through yonder window and so on and so on. It was daylight.

She was already up and out of bed. She brought in a tray with one of those old-fashioned French stovetop espresso makers and a couple of flowered cups. 'Coffee?'

'Thanks. Wonderful.'

'How do you take it?'

'Black,' he said, even though he liked sugar in it. That was how he remembered that she had preferred it.

'That's easy,' she said and poured some into his cup. 'I have to go to work, but you can stay in bed if you like.'

The absurd idea occurred to him that he could stay there, not even getting dressed, and still be here that evening when she got home from work. That would be presumptuous of course—but didn't she want him to presume? Was she perhaps inviting it? Supposing he did something like that and this encounter turned into something protracted, could that work? Was he good enough for her now? (Had he ever been?) He knew himself well enough to realize that she would be the one who would have to indicate what she wanted.

'No, I'll come downtown with you.'

'The car will be here in twenty minutes,' she told him. He got up and dressed as quickly as he could.

'Use my toothbrush if you want, she told him.'

He was unable to keep from wondering whether this was another gesture of intimacy or this was her habit with other casual lovers. He disapproved of the thought (although he had not been able to help himself). Still, his reaction wasn't jealousy but regret. This was yet another piece of evidence that he should have married her. Not just for his sake, but for hers. With him—who knows? —she might have had a happier, more protected life.

THE LIMO WAS WAITING at the curb in front of her building. They got in and he marveled at how she had restored herself to the professional perfection of the previous day. Hair, make-up—she didn't even look tired.

He tried to think of what to say. No more apologies, of course. Something forward looking, some expression at least of gratitude and amazement? That would be unnecessary, he hoped, but there should be some expression of appreciation that didn't sound moronic. It had been wonderful to feel like a twenty-year-old again, but there was also the awkwardness.

He took her hand and held it. That couldn't be misinterpreted. And expressed his feelings as well as any words could have done.

As they approached her building he said at last, 'I've got to go back to Albuquerque to tie up a few loose ends. But I'll call you.'

'No,' she said, 'don't.'

'Don't call?' he asked, not quite comprehending. And then, a beat later, 'Ever?'

'No.'

He couldn't argue with her, not there in the car with the driver in front. He had no idea what to do or to say.. Complain? Beg? Was she dismissing him? It seemed so.

'I don't understand,' he said at last.

'It will come to you,' she said. 'Trust me.'

Whatever the hell that meant.

The car pulled over to the curb. She got out. He got out. It was a cruelly dazzling morning.

'But I love you,' he blurted out as they stood there on the sidewalk.

'Yes, I know,' she said and kissed him on the cheek. She turned away and he watched her disappear into the revolving door.

3

'SO? SO WHAT DO YOU THINK?'

What do I think about what?

'The story. That's it. There isn't any more.'

That's ridiculous. That wasn't an ending. If I'm going to be the narrator, you've got to give me something else.

'I never saw her again. Or spoke to her. What else could there be? That was it. Or almost.'

How 'almost'?

'On the plane home I was sure that it had been revenge, something she had to have been fantasizing and planning for a long time. She had no idea that we would meet at the TV station but she was all ready. I don't know. It's possible, I suppose, that she was expecting to see me, because she knew the producers and might have asked who else was on the schedule. But I was convinced that she was as surprised as I was and that she was dumping me this way after such a great night, because I had dumped her years before. It seemed... just. And part of me was willing to admit that I'd deserved it. But mostly I couldn't believe it of her. Was she the kind of person who holds grudges that long? Leah, maybe, but her? On the other hand, did I know her well enough even to make such a judgment? I loved her and I had no idea what to think, but couldn't stop thinking.'

And?

'And, and, and. I kept mulling it over for months and eventually came to a glimmer of useless understanding. It doesn't excuse anything but it was clarifying. I had been ashamed of myself for breaking up with her, but that had not been the worst of it. What I realized was that I had been ashamed of my parents. For the first time in my life, I saw them as fundamentally wrong. Not bigots, maybe, but with closed minds. And it is possible that my fear back then had been of a catastrophe worse than what I'd let myself imagine. Say that I'd talked with Jenny and we'd decided just to keep on going without any engagement or marriage (or even commitment). That fight with my parents would have happened eventually and I knew I'd lose. But the worry I had never admitted to myself was that, knowing how wrong-headed they were, I'd have wound up hating them. Their disowning me? That would have been unfortunate. My father was a rigid kind of man, but even so we might eventually have got to someplace where we could talk to one another. But my disowning them would have been worse and would have lasted longer, maybe forever.

'It's also possible, I guess, that I could have brazened it out. I could have stayed with Jenny and waited for them to make their objections, and then waited longer to see if they'd come around. I could have given them the chance to show a little compassion or reason. Or love. They did love me, in their smothering way. It wasn't a foregone conclusion that they'd behave as badly as I feared. That's a bothersome idea. What I like about it is that it makes them look better and me look worse—craven and spineless. It also distresses me to realize that I owed it to Jenny at least to try. She was an innocent bystander in all this. And that was insulting.'

I'm a narrator, not a shrink. Or a rabbi. But it sounds plausible. Still, isn't there anything else? What about Caroline, the woman you were living with?

'What about her?'

Did you mention any of this to her?

'Of course not. What would have been the point? To enjoy confessing? Most of the time, confession is just an excuse for bad manners and self-indulgence. Why burden her? And there was no practical use to her in having the information. I wasn't still seeing Jenny. Just thinking about her, and we are all entitled to our thoughts.'

But you had thought of leaving her?

'The idea crossed my mind, but would it have done her any good to know that? You think of suicide, maybe, but if you don't kill yourself, it's only a thought. And you keep it to yourself.'

You never called her? Or wrote? Jenny, I mean.

'She had told me not to. I was tempted and I'd think about it now and then. But I didn't want to annoy her. Besides, what could have happened? It's unlikely that she would have invited me to move in with her in New York. I'm not even sure I would have had the nerve to do it. You never outgrow pusillanimity, which seems to be a part of my character. But I didn't call or write and she never called me. She never extended that invitation.'

You and Caroline are getting on?

'Just fine. We had been fine before. Nothing changed. When Jenny died, I told Caroline that we had been in love as undergraduates. That was enough, wasn't it?'

'THREE OR FOUR YEARS LATER I saw her obituary in the *Times*. Actually, I didn't just come across it, reading the paper. Leah e-mailed me, which she almost never does, to call my attention it. And I suspect to gloat. Which I rather enjoyed, because it was maybe the first time she had alluded to Jenny in all that time or had admitted, even indirectly, that she had been jealous. As she should have been.

'But there it was in the paper. No picture but a respectable five paragraphs.

She died in Paris from complications of breast cancer. (Maybe Marie-Antoinette wasn't such a good name.) She was still young—in her middle fifties. I was still in love with her, of course, and I thought

79

of her pretty much the way I had before our great night. And afterwards. She was more elegant and regal than the 19-year-old girl I'd first known but she was the same woman. I had been proud of her, which makes no sense at all. But now I would never have another cup of black coffee with her. I wouldn't have had that anyway but there was a finality to this. It felt worse than the deaths of most of my blood relatives. That was when it came to me that revenge couldn't have been her intention. Not possible. She was too good for that.'

You're sure?

'Absolutely.'

What was that night about then?

'My guess? She wanted to keep us the way we had been. To go back, to remember us, and preserve us in amber. And she wanted to remind me, too, not to make me feel bad or good but just to revisit her youth and mine. I don't think she wanted me turn into an occasional lover who showed up from time to time like the saxophone player. And who knows how many other guys? I would have been happy to settle for that, but she wouldn't. If that was true, I had to admire her for her lofty standards. And it also followed that she loved me more than I ever knew. Only after she was dead did I begin to understand how much. I know it sounds extravagant but it was difficult to resist comparing us with those great renaissance stories of frustrated love—Petrarch and Laura or Dante and Beatrice. That night we spent together was her way of confirming, for herself and me, too, that we were what we had remembered.. Had we married or kept on seeing each other, even just occasionally, that perfection would have tarnished. It always does.'

You believe this? Or is this just the malign influence of literature? We're in the real world here, aren't we?

'What real world? There are questions to which reality has no adequate answers. That's why there is religion. That's why physicists have invented all those particles and other dimensions. It sounds irrational, I know, but reason has limits and sometimes is just confusing. The dead can ascend, if not to heaven then, at least in our imaginations, to some kind of refinement. A great line in *Messiah* says that this corruptible must put on incorruption. I'm not religious but that resonates. At any rate, I find it comforting to suppose that she forgave me, had forgiven me decades before, and was now acting out her fantasy, which wasn't of revenge but of sharing one more night with me.'

Maybe. It's your story.

'I wish it were. I've recently had an idea of an even more unpleasant possibility. As I've been pondering for this.... What? *Écriture?* There's another explanation for why Jenny might not have wanted to see me again.'

I have my guess. What's yours?

'I've been stupid—again, still—not to see it. She could have been reluctant to see me again because she was afraid that she'd fall in love with me again and that we'd pick up from where we'd been, which she didn't want to happen because she didn't trust me. It was a wonderful night but it she wouldn't let it lead anywhere because I might still be the same stupid son of a bitch she remembered, one she could love, maybe, but not like very much.

That, I'm afraid, sounds plausible.

'As I think back on it, I remember that the bar was where her company had an account. That made sense. It was close to her office and convenient and she was in publicity. Actually, she was the head of it. Back then, it would have been less awkward for her to pick up the check this way on business meetings: she wouldn't have had to mess with credit cards or cash. Anyway, I didn't have a chance to pay. And then she paid for the cab with what she said was an allowance they gave her, which also might have been true. But she wouldn't let me pay for dinner either. And then the car in the morning was on the company, so I wasn't able to contribute a dime. I can't help thinking, that she was demonstrating that she was the hostess and I was the guest. And keeping me at a distance.'

I'd wondered about that.

'Then there was one last thing that happened, a message from the ether, or so it seemed. A dozen years later, more or less, I saw the obituary of the saxophone player. His had a picture. He was a dapper guy, a sharp dresser with one of those thin mustaches across the upper lip. He wasn't any Charlie Parker or John Coltrane, but he wasn't at all bad. I listened to a couple of his recordings and he was what I guess they call cool. Dreamy and contemplative with long lines of high notes that seemed to come from some trance-like state. He would probably have been better known if he hadn't spent half the year in Europe. Or maybe his style was just too cerebral to appeal to a wide audience. I don't know much about these things.

'I had expected to feel jealousy as I read about him and then for quite a while stared at his picture, but I didn't. Instead, I saw that he could have been Jenny's toy. An accessory like a good bag or a scarf or string of pearls. Exotic, perhaps, like a tame puma you sometimes see on a leash on Fifth Avenue. I admired her taste. She'd spent time in Africa, and in Paris, after all. He knew her longer than I did, surely, and they had a nice, convenient arrangement, but I was struck by the idea that it wasn't what she and I felt for each other. He was married and had a wife in Vienna, which Jenny hadn't mentioned. Why would she? If he was just an amusement, that detail wouldn't have been important. I don't know how I knew this but I did. I mean, forgetting that he was black, how seriously can one take a saxophone player? Even one who'd won some prizes.

'I remembered my surprise when I'd seen his ridiculous hat in her hallway. She had closets and there would have been less prominent places to keep it, but this had to be an announcement to me and maybe to other callers that she was taken and that we were not to presume or imagine anything long-term.

'It also crossed my mind that if she could play around for years with a black jazz musician, why couldn't she have played around with a Jew? For years. Forever. She'd have been willing. I'd have been delighted, I think. I hope. What she couldn't understand was the limit of my imagination.'

You think it could have lasted?

'No idea. In my youth and naivety I could have been annoyingly possessive, which would again have been my inadequacy, my fault. But maybe she could have managed me, you know? Brought me up a little. What it comes down to is that I probably just wasn't good enough for her.'

You said it, not me.

'Listen, Kacew, I know that. But even so, maybe she'd have been willing to settle.'

There was nothing to say that wouldn't have made him feel worse.

He was silent for a while and then said, à propos of nothing at all: 'I remember her breath on my shoulder that night. It was wonderful then. Now it's heartbreaking.'

But you never lived with her, did you?

'No. And maybe that was a good thing.'

And a moment later, 'Isn't love always delusional?'

'MORE THAN THAT. Sane people have delusions. But there's a category beyond that, I think. Derangement, I suppose I'd call it.'

You're claiming a lot.

'Yes, but then I've had this weird idea that has stayed with me for much of the time we've been working together. I'm not at all sure I want it in the book.'

Then why are you telling me. I'm a narrator, remember. I narrate.

'You also help me understand.'

An unintended consequence. That isn't my job.

'I know. Still, I think about her, with longing of course. I know she's dead but I imagine her body and am greedy to possess it. Not just her external appearance or even her orifices, but inside. If I could unzip the skin and enter her body, there'd be all these lovely viscera and organs, shining as I imagine them, and I can visualize myself kissing them, licking them, nuzzling and touching them. And not just her sexual organs but all of them, which seem eroticized,. Or at least they are all connected with her brain, her spirit. What I'm trying to do is to go beyond what we call private parts be in touch with parts of her that are really private—her glistening liver and her pancreas and purple, fist-shaped -spleen. I want to gaze at her cute little adrenals nestled in their capsules of fat. Really to know her, in more than the biblical sense. As much as I can, I want to live there. Absurd, of course, but as Einstein said, if an idea isn't absurd then there's no hope for it. I read that on a Starbuck's cup, I think. Which is also absurd.'

It's bizarre, I tell him. And it verges on disgusting.

'I know. But it isn't disgusting to me. There's a wonderful passage in Ovid's 'Remedies for Love' when he suggests that the lover who wants to get over his fascination with a woman should seek out her most unattractive moments and contemplate them. My thought would be that if such a maneuver worked, the man would not have been sufficiently in love for him or Ovid or us to worry about.'

He falls silent, which is just as well. And what is it you want me to do with this, I ask him?

'I have no idea. Just… take it into account.'

Not my métier, I'm afraid. That would be up to readers, if there are any. Let us be modest and say putative readers. There won't be very many, I'm suspect. The upside of that is that you don't have to worry about embarrassing yourself before the world. That world will be a couple of hundred people.

HE ASKS ME WHAT I THINK of it, not in terms of sales but from a purely literary standpoint, if there is such a thing. What can I do but tell him the truth? Narrators can sometimes mislead readers but they ought to be straightforward with their protagonists. (Unless the narrators are really weird, which I have always wanted to be but never had the nerve to try.) I tell him that it isn't bad, but he could get up off his ass and go to the alumnae office (which I guess is the alumni office now, with co-education), find her yearbook, and jog his memory a little by looking at her picture. At least do that. He agrees.

Don't do me any favors, I tell him. But if you want to convince me that you were in love, that'd be a start. Doesn't it strike you as astonishingly lazy not to? He admits this is true and walks over to the alumni office (it's not far) to inspect her senior year yearbook and look at her photo. But her picture is missing. (Maybe she was out of town that day, or just didn't care anymore about this school stuff.)

I have another idea. I look up her sister on the Internet. Her married name had been mentioned in that *Times* obit as one of the surviving relatives. Without too much difficulty, I find her telephone number and address in Manhattan and tell him to call her. He is nervous about it but does as he's told. She picks up on the fourth ring.

'Marcia?'

'Yes, who is this?'

He gives his name.

'From fifty years ago?'

'Closer to sixty.'

There's a pause and then she asks, 'What can I do for you?'

'Do you have a picture of Jenny?'

'Yes.'

'Could you send it to me?' he asks. To explain himself, he tells her, 'We were in love all those years ago. I should have married her.'

'Would she have married you?' (Skepticism in the voice? Or is it a not-so-veiled insult?)

'I don't know. I think so. At least we should have played out the hand to see where it got us.'

'You were both very young.'

Is she excusing him? Or is it just an observation?

'Not anymore,' he tells her. 'And I know better now. She was the love of my life, as the phrase goes.'

Silence.

'Was she happy?' he asks.

'Who is happy?' Marcia asks. 'She had happy moments. Like everyone.'

'Her marriage?'

'Well, they divorced, didn't they?'

'But some of it was good?'

'What is it you want of me?' she asks, now sounding a bit impatient. 'Or of her?'

'I want to hear that her life was okay at least for a while.'

'I suppose so. They traveled a lot. The both liked that.'

She waited for the next question while he got up the nerve to ask it. 'And the saxophone player? Were they in love?'

'How would I know?

'You're her sister. You would have had some sense of it.'

Silence for a few seconds. Clearly, she was deciding whether to go on with this or hang up on him.

Then: 'Not gaga in love, I don't think. They were too old for that. But it was pleasant. She admired him as a musician. He wasn't around all that much.'

'Can I come down to New York and take you to lunch? We could talk. I have lots more questions.'

'I don't think so,' she said, and then, 'You know, for years, you were the family villain.'

For years? Even after she married what's-his-name? (Douglas?) Was that what she'd meant? He tried not to sound pleased. 'But you'll send me the picture?'

'Yes, send me an email.' She gave him her email address. 'I'll get it to you.'

'Deeply grateful.'

'I was just going out. I've got to run.'

She sounded just like Jenny, the same careful elocution, the same low voice.

He turned the phone off, put it back on its stand and stared at it.

WHAT MORE PERSUASIVE EVIDENCE could there be? Of course she had loved him! If she had been only mildly hurt, his villainy couldn't have lasted so long. A month? Two? He was sorry to have been hated but glad to have been loved. Glad to have lasted 'for years.'

I had more than halfway expected—even hoped—that the entire book might turn out to be a Nabokovian romp, in which the protagonist just gets it wrong—as in *Despair*, in which the Doppelganger looks nothing at all like the fellow who murders him and tries to assume his identity. The world is full of such improbabilities; it's fiction that tends to be too cautious and reasonable. Authors don't want to put off their readers, but God has no such worries and does as he pleases. Who is going to edit him?

Our sad-sack protagonist could have misinterpreted that night with her in New York and his sentimental regrets would then have been little more than fantasies. Or cruel jokes. Leah, Caroline, and the world are there; Jenny isn't.

I asked him how he felt about it, learning this way that he'd been right and that she really had loved him.

'I adored her,' he said. 'And she loved me back. I'd have preferred that she had loved me less and had been hurt less.' A beat. 'I think I would have. I am not a villain. I was wrong back in college, but people make mistakes all the time. She survived. So did I.'

Can you forgive yourself?

'Forgive myself? Forgive my parents? At this point, what difference does it make? I'm old. They're dead. So is she. Still....'

Still?

'She was amazing. Wonderful. I finally got the picture from Marcia and I saw how beautiful she was. It was unnerving. I'd remembered her more or less but in sixty years or even twenty details blur. Her hair, for instance, was lots fluffier than I would have thought. It looked at the same time windblown and elegant. The photograph had been taken in the living room of her apartment, and I studied it but couldn't remember a thing. It was as if I'd never been there.

And then, of course, I realized I hadn't been. Not in the living room I mean. The hall, the kitchen, the bedroom, the bathroom, but never the living room.'

Some narrators would want to do something with that living room thing, you know. It's exactly right, given the history of the relationship. But I'll leave that to perceptive readers and trust them.

'She's smiling. Her eyes are slightly narrowed, as if she was considering something. Or reacting to a joke that was funny but not funny enough. I must have told her some jokes like that. Or I could have been one of those jokes.'

She was unlikely to have been thinking about you when the photograph was taken.

'Of course she wasn't. But she's gone and I'm here and this is the photograph Marcia sent me. So I can read it as having somehow been intended for me.'

You're a mystic now?

'No. Never mind. The face is slightly narrower than I'd remembered. She looked a little like Greer Garson, which is somewhere between beautiful and handsome. Very finely chiseled features, even in her fifties. But the details don't matter so much as the almost overwhelming feeling I have of loss. I can only look at the picture for so long and then my eyes close. I can't believe I was stupid enough to have let her go.'

As Marcia said, you were young.

'What does that matter? The fact remains, as plain as the smile on her face, that my life has been a mistake.'

Nonsense. That's melodramatic posturing. And it isn't what you really think, most of the time.

'Maybe not. But some of the time. Sometimes. And it still hurts.'

That, I can believe.

DAVID R. SLAVITT was born in White Plains, New York, in 1935, and educated at Andover, Yale, and Columbia. A poet, translator, novelist, critic, and journalist, he is the author of more than one hundred works of fiction, poetry, and poetry and drama in translation. He is also coeditor of the *Johns Hopkins Complete Roman Drama in Translation* series and the *Penn Greek Drama Series*. His honors include a Pennsylvania Council on Arts award, a National Endowment for the Arts fellowship in translation, an award in literature from the American Academy and Institute of Arts and Letters, and a Rockefeller Foundation Artist's Residence. He lives in Cambridge, Massachusetts, and has taught at Columbia, Princeton, Bennington, and the University of Pennsylvania.